Legends

A Literary Journal
From Grey Wolfe Publishing

2015 Edition

Edited by Diana Kathryn Plopa

Grey Wolfe Publishing, LLC
PO Box 1088
Birmingham, Michigan 48009
www.GreyWolfePublishing.com

© 2016 Grey Wolfe Publishing
Published by Grey Wolfe Publishing, LLC
www.GreyWolfePublishing.com
All Rights Reserved

ISBN: 978-1628281149
Library of Congress Control Number: 2015921349

Legends

Grey Wolfe Publishing's
Literary Journal
2015 Edition

Edited by Diana Kathryn Plopa

Legends is a literary journal produced by Grey Wolfe Publishing.

Each year, talented writers from around the globe lend their work to this showcase of short stories, essays and poems for your reading enjoyment.

Some of the stories and poems within these pages may help you revisit memories you thought you'd forgotten. Others may reawaken emotions long dormant. And still others may reacquaint you with the laughter of your childhood. Regardless of which piece of poetry or prose you find most appealing, we are certain that these authors will quickly become some of your new favorites.

Grey Wolfe Publishing is an independent publishing house, headquartered in Michigan. We are committed to walking through the paths of the publishing forest with our authors as equals; never leading, never following... always side-by-side, with the strength and confidence of the Pack.

Ni Bóna Na Coróin.

Acknowledgements

The production of this book each year could not be accomplished without the expertise, literary passion and dedication of our amazing Pack. Each is a writer as well as a company team member; and each lends their unique perspective to serve both the company and our authors with integrity and creativity. We are grateful for their daily contributions to the growth of the Pack.

Contents

1.
A Fascination
Diana Kathryn Plopa

Treading softly upon the floor
Aiming carefully but missing my mark
The boards creek and you awaken

Your long slender body arches upward as your
Wondrous eyes pierce my soul ... The walls around us echo
The silence of the many before us
Who have been as we are now ... Helpless and lost ... Drowning
In a sea of expectation

Several minutes pass as we stand together
Though we never touch ... Locked in our gaze
Is what comes next

I move a moment closer, yet once again, Caught in my tracks
A light shines from someplace deep inside you
It begs me to come closer ... But warns of hidden dangers
Within your power

Afraid ... I turn to go
For I am uncertain of what you could unlock in me

You catch me again
Your eyes won't release me ... Your soul won't release me
Your power holds me strong ... Drawing me again to you
A breeze floats through the room ... Yet all is still
The silence is so deafening
The light in you grows stronger ... I am powerless against it

You bring me in closer ... Deeper into that part of you
Where you hide your secrets ... And your strengths
Our souls collide in a cascade of colors
Melting together in a timeless dance of eternal oneness
Together we create a single spark
The universe vibrates with exhilaration

As our flame ignites
We realize now ... We are one ... At least in this way ... Forever
A fascination forged in steel
And hardened through ... Something ... Encapsulated in us

At last you relinquish your hold
And I slip away into the darkness ... Dew falls on my face
A warm wind blows through my heart
And I recall the words ... Once released but never forgotten
The night wraps around me ... Like too many old movies
I stroll the old places ... And think of you

2.
A Serving of Sweet Justice
Christopher Chagnon

Bucky McLean sat on the edge of his bunk, hung over, his greying hair strewn like blow-down swamp cedars, his face bruised with dried blood crusted in the corner of his mouth, as though he'd been in a fight. He had been in a fight. It was coming back to him now, while he searched the concrete floor for a memory. The concrete revealed, "Oh yeah. The Metropole Bar, and twenty beers or so, and countless shots a' tequila I pounded down last night," came into his mind, like a boat anchor being raised off the bottom of a mucky lakebed. He brushed the crust from his lips with his swollen left hand, and peered at the red flakes. "Fight? Oh yeah, some guy named Billy Briggs. That sonovabitch hit me!" He noticed the cut on the humps of his knuckles, "I got 'em back... I think?" The concrete spoke more of the memory, "What ta hell were we fighting about? Oh yeah, Nigger Larry. Why would that guy get so pissed about Nigger Larry?"

"You up now, ay?" Sheriff Lyman Brewmeister said, with a clank of a tin coffee cup hitting the paint chipped bars on Bucky's cell.

"Yaaa..." Bucky dragged his reply through a deserved yawn, "Time is it?"

"Ten in the morning."

Bucky gleaned the cell for other occupants. A couple of guys huddled in orange suits, like his, on twin bunks with their backs to him. The upper bed held Jim Ballard, a lithe pulpwood cutter (when he worked) from Millersburg. Probably brought in for back child support—the usual. The lower bunk contained some guy named Joe, ordinary Joe. He didn't recognize him. The floor was strewn with McDonald breakfast sandwich wrappers, "I miss the egg McMuffin's again?"

"Yeah, but I saved you a couple," the sheriff replied.

"Alright. You sonzabitches are alright!" Bucky laughed.

The sheriff squeezed two paper wrapped bundles, and the coffee though the narrow bars. "Sokay, Bucky. You know I wouldn't forget you, after all, it's your special day."

Bucky stood, stretched, and fetched the sandwiches. "My special day? Indeed. Sue's gonna' be pissed. It's her birthday. Did she call yet?"

"Yeah, she's on her way."

"What's the charge this time, drunk and disorderly? Fighting? Profanity in a public place?"

"All of the above, and a few others, ta' boot," the sheriff revealed.

"A few others?" Bucky wasn't sure what they could be. The others were the usual charges.

"Seems Mr. Briggs is pressing for an assault charge, too. Another is property destruction. You broke a bar table, and a couple 'a bar stools. The guy says you did something else, you might be charged with racial intimidation."

"I didn't break 'em by myself, that other asshole was right with me, ya' know?" Bucky protested. "Ay, you know if I won the fight? What the hell is racial intimidation?"

The sheriff spoke, "Probably. If Briggs thought he'd won there wouldn't be any assault charges, I bet. He's some kind a' Union do-gooder from downstate. He works in the Civil Rights department at Solidarity House. I don't know a thing about racial intimidation; apparently it's a new law. Ya' can't call people niggers, Bucky."

Bucky coddled his swollen hand, and rubbed his bruised cheek, "That's what he is, he knows it." Bucky touched his bruise again, "You sure I won? Don't feel like it. Where's the other guy? Didn't he get busted, too?"

"No, he didn't. He was more convincing than you last night. You'll see the judge this afternoon. Eat yer McMuffins, Bucky." The sheriff noticed the mess on the floor, "Ay, you sonzabitches, clean that shit up."

Bucky ate his breakfast. The sheriff walked back to the dispatcher's desk, while the two napping inmates stirred to wake on their bunks.

Ordinary Joe began picking up. "I ain't pickin' yer shit up," he said to Ballard.

"Never asked ya' to, asshole," Jim Ballard said, when he reached the floor from the upper bunk. He stood glaring down at Joe who was a foot shorter.

"Jus kiddin'," Joe Fern said, below the sight of the impressive logger.

"Ay, pick this up, too, ya' wad," Bucky said, throwing his wrappers in a far corner of the cell. Bucky was a seasoned cell occupier, king of the roost in the Presque Isle County jail. He knew, immediately, he didn't like the guy named Joe. "You don't come into my cell and start givin' orders," Bucky warned the newcomer.

Joe Fern retreated, and said nothing.

"Ay, Bucky?" Jim Ballard greeted respectfully. Ballard knew Bucky was king in the cell. He knew Bucky was somewhat of a king on the outside, too, after working with him in the woods over the years. Ballard was a tough brawler, but he knew Bucky possessed a lot of heart, a lot of sand, and a lot of steam to go with it. The kind of stuff that makes you well known, and makes people whisper when you walk past them. Bucky, definable, was not someone to mess with.

"Jim Ballard," Bucky pronounced, "you in for the usual, I suppose?"

"Yeah, the old lady got me busted again. There ain't no work right now. I've been off for a couple a' months," he kicked a wrapper, "mill's been shut down, too."

"You ever go see Curtis? He's lookin' for pulp cutters, like I tole you."

"Hah," Ballard laughed, "hunting season's here. Who wants ta' work in deer season?"

"Lazy fucker! No wonder why yer' in here. Get off yer' lazy ass," Bucky slammed the dead-beat father of two.

"Well, I sure will as soon as the judge lets me out," Ballard said, but didn't protest Bucky's blunt delivery of fact.

"Guess what? Yer ass is gonna be sittin' right here through deer season. Judge ain't gonna let you out right away. Dumb ass."

"Yeah, yeah, I know. I'm a dumb ass," Ballard conceded.

Thirty-year-old Joe Fern went back to his bunk, and kept to himself while Bucky and Ballard talked about working in the woods. This was Fern's first incarceration. It was doubtful he was arrested for fighting, given his frail tendencies, and lackluster physical attributes. After listening to his cell partners discuss the many times they joined each other in the county jail, he thought it time to reveal why he was put behind the flakey, yellow painted bars. He brushed the wisp of oily brown hair from his eyes, and tried to join in. "This is my first time."

"First time for what?" Bucky sniggered, not caring for the slight intrusion.

"Behind bars."

"You want some sort a medal, or something? Ain't something to be proud of," Bucky scoffed.

"Hell, I kinda like it here. They'll feed me, and I hear they gotta get ya' fixed if yer sick. I got a bad toothache, I'm gonna' tell 'um, too. The law says they gotta' pay for it. I ain't got no job, no insurance. I'll let the County take care a' me for a while."

"Boy, ain't you somethin' a mother would be proud of? You ever had a job?" Bucky said, disgusted, insulted.

"Nope."

"Just shut the fuck up, and stay that way. If I wanna' hear from ya' I'll pull yer chain," Bucky warned.

Joe Fern slid himself to rear of his bunk, "Sorry, just sayin'."

"You believe that guy? I know yer lazy, but that dick is

beyond yer unemployment, I mean unenjoyment, check takin' ass," Bucky laughed. So did Ballard.

Ballard changed the subject, "How's Sue?"

"Probly mad as a wet hen right now. It's her birthday, and I promised I'd take her shoppin'. I'll have to use her birthday money ta make bail now. Maybe I can work out a deal with Judge Bartlett for community service again." Bucky studied his favorite spot on the floor, "I miss my little daughters, already."

"Too bad for her, and the kids. Community service, that's the only way I can pay, too," Ballard confided, "They had me cleaning street gutters the last time. It wasn't bad. I found ten bucks stuck in a drain grate. But the deputy made me cough it up towards my fine. What an asshole."

The steel entry door leading to the jail cells opened, and thirty years a bailiff, Harold Warren, stopped at their cell, "Inmate Ballard, the judge will see you in court for arraignment. Face the bars for the chains." Ballard was chained at his wrists and feet.

"Don't take any shit from the judge now," Bucky said, behind a sly grin.

"I know better than to sass her. She's a hangin' judge."

Bucky giggled, "Just messin' with ya'."

Bucky settled on the long approach of his bunk, and studied the bedsprings of the upper bunk. Joe Fern lay, anxiously, wanting to tell Bucky of his unlawful deed that put him in the County jail, his act of validation. Without invitation, he began telling Bucky the sordid details with great delight.

Bucky listened, and cringed. The pillow he placed over Joe Fern's face subdued the agonizing cries and screams as Bucky set upon the cellmate with a great deluge of fists and feet. Bucky didn't cease his attack until he heard the steel door opening down the dimly lighted hallway leading to his cell. It was Sheriff Brewmeister. "Time to see the judge, Bucky."

Bucky washed the blood from his hands, and followed the sheriff. Joe Fern lay motionless below his pillow.

Protocol called for a prisoner to be bound in chains when led to the courtroom. Not Bucky, though. He was trusted, and well-liked by the department. After all, he was their best customer, and king of the jail cell.

The sheriff took Bucky to the department's lobby, not the usual way to the courtroom. A crowd of deputies, dispatchers, and staff had assembled in anticipation of Bucky's arrival. Dispatcher, Mary Henning, made one of her popular Sweet Justice cakes for the event. 'Congratulations' icing was scripted on its top. It was displayed on her desk. The gathered participants clapped, and congratulated Bucky with back patting, handshakes and cheers.

"What's goin' on here?" Bucky said, surprised. "Why is everyone saying' congratulations? Did I win the lottery, or something?"

Cake was served with coffee.

Magistrate Gordon stepped forward, "On behalf of the staff, and the County of Presque Isle, I'd like to congratulate you on your robust achievement. Your latest incarceration has set a new County record. Sixty, yes, sixty times you've been arrested and housed in this fine institution. It's a new record, Bucky."

The applause continued while the magistrate presented Bucky with an ancient skeleton key that was spray-painted with cheap, gold paint.

Bucky, humbled by the affection, and his ignoble record, bowed and said, "Thank you. It's been a pleasure, and I've worked hard to achieve it, my friends."

Sheriff Brewmeister called out, "Okay everyone, party's over. Bucky, let's go, the judge is waiting."

When they reached the courtroom, Sue was sitting in the audience, humbled, embarrassed and broke. Judge Bartlett read Bucky's charges, like she had fifty-nine times in the past. When she reached the charge of 'Racial Intimidation' she removed her glasses, and examined the prosecutor, "Am I reading this correctly?"

The prosecutor shuffled a stack of papers on his table, "Yes, your Honor. We are charging Mr. McLean with the new law. A man's civil liberties have been violated. He was involved in a brawl, used profanity and racial intimidation last night in the Metropole Bar."

The judge glared at Bucky from her bench. "What do you have to say in your defense, Bucky... Mr. McLean?"

Bucky squeezed his gold key under the table, "I don't know what the big fuss is all about? I was talkin' to Nigger Larry," Bucky turned to search the audience where he saw Billy Briggs sitting in a far corner. His swollen right eye bore witness to the altercation, "PRIVATELY!" his voice rose. "That is until that asshole, I mean, gentleman got all jacked and took a swing at me. See? Hit me right there," Bucky pointed to his cheek. Briggs squirmed in his chair. "What was I ta' do, Judge? Take an ass whoppin'? I don't remember much after that."

Judge Bartlett called the prosecutor to her bench where they whispered legalese. "Will the defendant please rise?"

Bucky stood, still clutching his key.

"You are charged with the following." She read the charges. "Your bail is set at one thousand dollars. Can you post bail at this time, Mr. McLean?"

Bucky dropped his key where it pinged on the hardwood floor. "No, your Honor, I can't. I guess I'll have to stay in jail. Sorry."

Sitting amongst the audience was a dark-skinned man of Louisiana Creole descent. He left his chair, and asked if he could address the bench.

"Is there something you can contribute to this case, Sir?"

The dark-skinned man with sunset eyes said, "Mais, oui," and waved a thousand dollars in his raised hand. "I was theyah'. In dat bah, I mean, when the fight broke out. Me and Bucky was jus minin' are biness when this otha' fella starts ta fussin', and gettin' all upsets. He hits po' Bucky reah' hah'd. Ain't no call fah' 'at, I says, ya' Honah. Me 'n Bucky's reah gut friens, ain't no call fah 'at, yaz' ax' me? I come ta' pay Mistah Bucky's bail."

The judge studied the man, trying to decipher his crypt dialogue. "Are you saying Mr. McLean didn't start the fight? You want to post bail for him?"

"At's wad' I'm talkin' 'bout, ya' Honah."

"Did you hear Mr. McLean utter any racial slur to anyone? Or call anyone a, please excuse my having to repeat this, nigger?"

"Mais, yes, ya' Honah.   That's what he calls me."

"So.   He did use a racial epithet while referring to you?

"I'm not so shuah 'bout no epatats.   Mais, shuah, he call me niggah."

The judge, now bewildered, fussed about her throne, trying to find something significant to adjust while she considered the stranger's defense of the accused Bucky.   "Okay, for the record, could you please state your full name?"

"I be obliged, ya' Honah.   My name is Niggah Larrah'.   Dass all, Niggah Larrah'.   And me an' Bucky's frens'.   Bucky, he mon ami."   Nigger Larry reposed apologetically,   "Oh, I knoz' what cha' thinkin'.   Me havin' ta' be called niggah.   Well, ya' see when I was enfant I was reah cream-skin likes ya'll.   Coonass.   Maw-maw don't wan' no mistake made, so she names me Niggah, soz me, and everyone else make no mistakes.   Ya' see, ya' Honah?"

After great protests and pleas from the prosecutor to keep some of the charges against Bucky McLean intact, and Billy Briggs huffing out of the court room, the award winning incarcerate was set free.

Sheriff Brewmeister led Bucky, and Jim Ballard back to the jail.   Bucky was released.   Jim Ballard was returned to his cell where Joe Fern coiled beneath a blanket, barely alive.   "Fern, your turn to face the judge," Brewmeister called out.

Joe Fern didn't move.   He groaned in agony.   The sheriff removed his covering, "What the hell happened to you?"

Fern couldn't reply; his jaw was broken and his eyes were swollen shut.   The sheriff hustled down the hallway to call an ambulance to take Joe Fern to the hospital.   But Joe Fern got his wish, and didn't have to worry; Presque Isle County would have to pay his medical expenses.   Even child molesters were covered by the County's insurance.

3.
A Sore Loser
Diana Kathryn Plopa

She was everything her mother had told her not to be, and still, it hadn't made a difference. Raised in a highly conservative family with the tumult of propriety everywhere she turned, it was difficult to win. She dressed well, had impeccable manners, and a dowry large enough to capture preeminent suitors... and still, it wasn't enough. She wanted something more, something different.

One day, he came to her door, roses in one hand, and a proposal of marriage in the other. Of course, her parents approved; he was from good stock, and had a bank balance that mirrored his social standing. He was the finest champagne of men, oozing refinement and promising a life of forever bliss. In her soul, she knew it was a scam, but went along anyway; accepting the loss of any individuality she may have attained had she played the game differently.

Three years later, they had two delightful children, and a nanny to care for them. She pranced the social scene unencumbered by poverty or guilt, making good use of charity to fill her lost evenings. He immersed himself in his work and was rarely present – physically, emotionally, spiritually, sexually or in nearly every other way – except financially. It's what kept her content. And still, it wasn't enough. She wanted something more, something different. She'd lost the teenage fantasy of her white knight; and she had accepted that loss with the daily immersion of false prophets who regaled her with the hint of emancipation through prayer, wine and tolerance. The affect was only slightly comforting.

Twenty years passed. The children had grown and moved on to take up residence in the finest Universities of Europe, chasing dreams and catching rainbows. Each found a path of least resistance, which also provided for some modicum of joy and success. They weren't yet satisfied – but they were working at it, fervently. She envied their opportunity and courage. She'd lost all of that with the acceptance of a rose on the veranda of a summer afternoon.

She remained at home, fighting off the jealousies of women who floated ghost-like through her marriage; never truly discovering her path of least resistance. Agitation and quiet rage, she came to understand, could not compete with the undulation of apathy or the small flame of happiness she dared to reach for; the singe of its heat eluding her. She wanted nothing more. She'd lost the spark.

When he died tragically, on a ferry while commuting home from his latest lover's chateau, of a brain aneurism, she did not weep for him. Why should she? She'd lost the continuance she'd been dependent on for thirty years; and she was irritated that he'd left her the burden of their vast estate. There were lawyers to handle the delicate complications, of course; but she was saddled with the annoyances of the daily ills of maintenance. She'd lost the recumbent lifestyle to which she had become accustomed. She was on her feet now, more than was comfortable; a telephone relentlessly dangling within reach as she was forced to make decisions, choose paths that could never relinquish resistance, and parent her grown children a continent away.

She resented all he had left her. She resented all he had done to keep her placid over the decades they'd been together. She resented the plans she was now forced to make in order to preserve her children's entitlement program. She'd never wanted any of this. Now that she'd lost the key to her self-loathing with no target of amiable anxiety, she resented herself.

The housekeeper found her a month after his death, her naked body draped with the jewels of his false remorse; her head lying on a pillow of the pages of his portfolio, stained with the blood of her awareness.   She'd left the world lost in a sea of heaving self-doubt.   She'd had it all, she'd lost nothing tangible, only the love she never possessed; and yet, she rallied against her privilege and resented the moment he'd left her with responsibility.

She hadn't coped with losing well.

4.
Ah Oklahoma, The Drama
Matt McGee

The stage was set. Aunt Eller's shack leaned on the left, a towering mass of balsa wood and two-by-fours that could be rotated when needed, turned into another shack. It had been loaned out from a prop house in La Verne about eighty miles away. It cost us $125 a day, or $1,400 for the whole run. "The place cost more than the rent on my actual apartment," I'd say, and people would tell me I needed to move to a better neighborhood. I'd look at the shack while the cast was rehearsing on stage and dream of sleeping in it, rent-free.

On the right was the windmill. With deliberately crooked fans and spokes it would turn with the flick of a switch at the right time during certain numbers. Laurey and her ensemble would stride in to do 'Surrey' or 'Cain't Say No'; I'd throw a switch from my podium and whoosh, instant Oklahoma breeze.

Trouble started early, in the first week of rehearsal actually. Brian, cast as Curley, was a burly kinda guy, more fit for pro wrestling than musical theatre. It isn't an easy role, physically demanding, requiring the actor to be limber enough to pull off complicated choreography.

William, the director, waved a pen and declared "I'm casting him anyway." We all heard the choreographer groan. The body he'd been assigned was made less for Broadway and more by Budweiser. And to his credit, Brian worked hard.

He ate hard, too. In fact, I'd never seen a rehearsal interrupted by a Dominos delivery man before. But one evening around dinnertime, down the aisle came a middle-aged man in a red and blue polo shirt he should've outgrown decades earlier. Brian spotted him, left his place mid-number and accepted a steaming cardboard box from the guy's hotbag. We looked on in stunned silence. Even the twenty percent tip didn't shock us back awake. If you work in the service industry and someone really good-looking doesn't tip you, chances are they're an asshole or an actor.

"What the... hell..." said Jud Fry, who was being played by a guy from the Valley, named Jud. He was the first one in costume (I heard a rumor he and the costumer were getting it on in the loft between acts). Jud was the first actor off-book, the first one in the parking lot on rehearsal nights and often the last to leave. He looked at Brian, who turned back to rehearsal, box in hand. "You've gotta be freakin' kidding me."

Curley-Brian opened the box. He pulled a slice out, stuffed it in his mouth then offered the open box to Jud-Jud. With a swift backhand Jud smacked the box from Curley's grip, sending it scattering up stage center. "Awwwww," Curley said. Then he went right back to his slice of pizza. Jud stepped in close enough that he could smell fresh pepperoni.

"Listen, fatass. I don't give a shit what you eat, or what you do on your own time. But this is my whole life. This is what I do. And I'm not gonna have some third-rate hack who can't dance for shit fuck it up for me."

Curley-Brian stopped chewing and locked eyes with Jud in a dead silent duel. Then Curley-Brian took the rest of the slice, folded it, and stuffed it into his mouth. He took a step closer to Jud-Jud and pressed his belly against the smaller man's chest. Another few inches and he could've knocked him over.

Curley-Brian took a few steps back, a bull ready to charge. Jud's knees bent. Members of the ensemble assembled onstage faster than if they'd actually been called; whispers shoot through a theatre green room like a tornado. They stared on from a healthy distance.

Brian stared Jud down. "Why don't you go clean the hen house, Jud."

A genuinely amused laugh sounded from the ensemble. Late arrivals thought it was an improv.

Jud squinted one eye and said, "what'd you say? What right you got beatin' up on a defenseless pizza like that?"

"You got something to say, Curley?"

"I should ask you the same thing. Have you got something to say, Jud?"

Jud's posture rose an inch or so, seeing the threat had lessened. "No, I think 'don't fuck up my performance, fatass' pretty much covers it."

Brian stared at Jud a moment more. Then he shrugged and said "well alright then" good-naturedly. He walked upstage, collected his pizza back into its box and prepared to stand upright and leave.

Jud-Jud wasn't having it. He'd followed Curley-Brian to the offended pizza and, just as it was almost collected, Jud kicked his left foot straight thru the box like David Beckham. This time, it splattered across Aunt Eller's chicken coop, except one piece that soared errantly into the rafters, came briefly back down and speared into one of the crooked blades of the windmill. We all looked up at it, dangling like limp, spoiled perfection.

Jud smiled his actor's polished, crooked smile, and those of us who have lived a few years leaning against bars, saw the fingers of Curley-Brian's right hand begin to form a tight, silent clench.

Laura, who was playing Laurey, rushed through the crowd, field dress aflutter and arms akimbo. "Boys! Boys stop this!" The ensemble looked at one another. Jud-Jud did what was expected of his character; he grabbed Laurey-Laura and shoved her to the ground, never moving his eyes from Curley-Brian.

Just as I was wondering who we had as a neutral party – a director, producer, someone, from the ranks of the ensemble stepped up. Patty, a hefty woman cast as Aunt Eller pointed a gun toward the rafters. The shot from her starter's pistol snapped everyone's shoulders a moment, turning attention her way. And hey, why not? It worked in Act II.

"Alright knock it off, boys!"

This worked as a temporary distraction, but unfortunately Patty was a daycare instructor and, consequently, sounded like one. No one took her tone seriously and a moment later, everyone went right back to what they were doing.

Failing the appearance of the production staff, and Aunt Eller's tried-and-true pistol trick having failed, I watched Curley-Brian and Jud-Jud lock eyes again. This time, they'd have to do something about it or look like a couple of pussies, and they knew it. Just as their feet started to march toward one another, I went back to thinking about how a neutral party ought to step in. Then I realized, "oh, right. That's me."

"OK GUYS LET'S BREAK IT UP. JAMES GET THAT PIZZA OFF MY FUCKING WINDMILL. LAURA, STOP LOOKING LIKE A WINSLOW HOMER PAINTING, GET YOUR ASS OFF MY STAGE. BRIAN! JUD!"

The two had broken their death stare. People began to lose interest and drift into the wings.

"Are you guys fucking deaf? I said get off my goddamn stage! You wanna brawl there's a nice big parking lot out back." I stepped away. They turned back to staring one another down. Then, Curley-Brian did what I didn't expect.

"Good idea. Let's go, Jud."

"Let's go," Jud agreed.

"Ah, Jesus Christ," I moaned, seeing the plan backfire. "Are you kidding me? WE'VE GOT A SHOW IN FORTY MINUTES."

"Good," said Jud. "That'll give fatty here thirty-nine minutes to compose himself after I give him the sixty second ass-kicking he's had coming for weeks."

Brian banged open the stage door. Night air rushed in across our brown Oklahoma plain. Jud went out first then Brian followed. Neither seemed interested in whether or not anyone was following.

Seeing no one else was going to make the decision I grabbed the door and slammed it shut behind them. The whole of the ensemble stood gawking; forty bodies in half make-up and partial costuming.

"JOSH. CHRIS. You guys understudied Curley and Jud."

"Yeah," they echoed together.
"You're promoted. Get in costume. Laura get with Josh and go through those dance moves, particularly the Dream sequence. Jud and Brian will have to stay outside and cool off. DAYNA!" The

sound engineer at the front of the house took off her headset. "DON'T LET THOSE TWO BACK IN MY BUILDING." She thumbs-upped me. I turned to the ensemble.

"If anyone else has a problem, I'm the guy to talk to. Those two want to make themselves look like idiots, they're going to be surprised at what their contracts say about professionalism. Now, GIT. Everyone! In costume and on stage, doors open in TWENTY MINUTES!"

One of Laura's ensemble said "thank you, twenty." The rest took it as a cue and echoed the same. Bodies turned and made for their dressing rooms.

Dayna had passed the word to security. Brian and Jud were kept from the building for the duration of the show which, if you didn't know the understudies were playing the principals, you'd never know the difference. And I heard Brian and Jud's talk was all bluster; security cameras revealed that soon after my closing it, the two joined forces to try and pry open the door. Then, banded together like the Defiant Ones, shackled by want-to-do-theatre, they began checking all entrances until they found an open one. Finally, turned away everywhere, they took to greeting the arriving crowd in the lobby.

"Howdy, welcome to our show!"

From an opera box, they watched Chris and Josh fill their boots. Brian and Jud, as they were now commonly known, spent intermission pleading their case. They used their acting skills on a couple of seventy year-old ushers, convincing them they'd been accidentally locked out and needed to get back in immediately. Once backstage, they were escorted back out the side door I'd sent them thru an hour earlier.

I'm told that, by the time the title number started, the duo had retired to The Yukon Belle across the street and buried their hatchet in a pitcher of Bud Light. They traded war stories of productions gone by on into the night, agreeing this would be a new story for their books. Ultimately, they sauntered back to the parking lot, to their unwashed economy cars and moseyed off, still in costume, toward separate homes in separate corners of town.

Meanwhile, Josh and Chris congratulated each other, post-show. Laura went home with Chris (there had been rumors of a show-mance). Brian and Jud arrived home too, half tipsy, each to flop onto their tired, warped mattresses. Neither were able to afford anything new on their actor's salary, a pay that would now be appropriately docked. They'd eventually close their eyes, fall into sleep, and dream the way that old gunslingers do when the day finally arrives that their draw is too slow, and the new hand comes to town to claim their rightful place.

5.
Anger and Grief:
Two Sides of the Same Coin
Diana Kathryn Plopa

"Anger suffers as grief withdraws." At least that's what my shrink told me as I clutched the pillow to my chest, watching the heartless snow fall upon his Cambridge window pane. He said, "Don't worry Amy, as your grief goes away, so will your anger; for the two cannot live without each other. They feed on each other. Grief soothes anger. Anger feeds grief. When you can bring yourself to let go of one, the other will also disappear. It's the simple nature of things."

As I wrote the check and dropped it in the competent hands of his secretary, I left that session with a new appreciation for life, death, anger, grief, and the stupidity of psychoanalysis.

Simply put, my Harvard educated, psych-babble wielding, one-hundred-dollar-per-hour egomaniac analyst was wrong. Good old Dr. What's It got it wrong. After the few brief months of the all-consuming grief of my mother's passing subsided, the anger remained... and in full force; albeit just under the surface of my daily life; irritating every thought, every decision, every joy.

Each day, I recalled the fact that my mother, with whom I had parted company on less-than-stellar terms, was no longer in my life. And I was still angry about the fact. I was angry that our last conversation together was not a pleasant one; and angry that she had refused to do anything to improve her situation in life... for years.

As I walked the snow-covered streets from the T-station back to my apartment on Boylston Street, I rehashed the frustration, reinvigorating the anger with each sloshing step of boot against icy pavement.   My mother had spent the last five years self-medicating and ignoring the advice of doctors; claiming, "They don't really know what they're talking about and clearly, I know my body much better than they do.   After all, I live with it every day."

Our heated phone call ended with my telling her, "After four years of medical school, four years of residency, and who knows how many years in practice affiliated with a top-rated hospital, you're going to question your cardiologist?"

She said, "I don't want to discuss this anymore." And there was silence on the line. She had hung up on her daughter. The whole thing was nuts! And so, without much fanfare, she died three weeks later. She had a heart attack on Easter morning. I didn't expect her resurrection, even though she had been baptized not many years before in the very same waters that John had dunked Jesus.

As the grief withdrew, the anger swelled within me, tainting my memory of her and the childhood we shared.   The anger that lingered made me question the happy memories I had of her... made me question my relationship with her... made me question– albeit briefly –my actions as a mother. I had vowed not to follow in her negative footsteps, and only resole the positive steps.   Would I do that? The anger of her passing made me question far too much. And the grief no longer consoles.

When I brought this inconsistency to the attention of dear Dr. What's It, all he could say was, "Everyone grieves differently, Amy.   Your process is unlike anyone else's."

Then why am I paying you ridiculous amounts of money each month to convince me there are rules to these things, and answers easily found if I sacrifice my most conflicting thoughts on your couch of absolution? That was the last time Dr. What's It and I spent any time together. I don't miss him, and I doubt he misses me.

It's been over a year now, and I've made peace with my anger... dislodged my grief... and subsisted on the understanding that we all do the best we can in this world... to get by. And for those who don't try, well, they get what they get; and we, sooner or later, become comfortable with our discomfort when reflecting on the aftermath.

6.
Beach on the Rocks
A.J. Huffman

Chunks of ice pile along shore's edge.
The thawing waves, force them out,
erode them slowly back into liquid form.
I have an urge to push several back in,
listen to them clink, cubes falling
into an over-sized highball.   The perfect
mix, a toast to rising warmth
of morning sun.

7.
Blue Monday
Mark Hudson

Some say Blue Monday is January 20,
and people are experiencing blues plenty.
Why does it fall on Martin Luther King's day?
It really seemed that the sky was so gray.
I went to the art institute with a teacher I know,
the topic was food of the display they shown.
It was interesting to see pictures of food on display,
but I also saw the homeless starving that day.
The exhibit was on dining, an American tradition,
feeding the hungry is such an urgent mission.
Why do people pay to see paintings of food?
Outside people beg and they're considered rude.
The Norman Rockwell thanksgiving scene can tell
that the past is gone, and the present is hell.
Paintings from the past represent a certain view,
and even back then they had Mondays quite blue.

8.
Caterpillars and Moths
Mark Hudson

Based on a story at East Tennessee wildflowers.com

This is a story supposedly true,
It's got some humor, and some blues,
A science teacher who taught fourth grade,
and photos of butterflies, caterpillars he made.
The caterpillars eat their shedding skin.
He went with his son to a grocery store,
and he saw a girl who had some moths in
a jar she held, the girl was about four.
He took a picture of the moths thanks to the kid,
he brought the photos to his class.
The kids were grateful for what he did,
but he told the students it would be his last
year he'd be teaching fourth grade,
the students were sad, but gave him thanks.
It was a hard choice he already made,
the teacher taught science despite their pranks.
One kid even claimed he wanted to be
a teacher one day thanks to the influence.
A science teacher from Tennessee,
spared these kids from being future truants.
The children will blossom like wildflowers,
but the teacher doesn't know what's next.
Education is what brings us power,
it makes us mightier than insects.

9.
Civil Wounds
Elizabeth Farney Maxson

The soldiers on the ground looked at the sky in anticipation. They knew a battle was forthcoming, but from which direction and how many soldiers were impossible to ascertain. Their own blue uniforms were stained with mud, gun powder, and blood from themselves and from fallen brothers around them. The reason to fight was clear, but victory seemed distant now. How could victory be possible when so many had to die to achieve it? Who were they killing? Surely, they were not fathers, sons, grandfathers, uncles, husbands, lovers, or friends to anyone. They were simply men with guns trying to kill everyone in their paths, and for what? To allow themselves the right to tell others that they had no rights?

Etta wasn't the first woman to hide behind the ranks and fight for the Union. She was, however, an extremely good shot. Her father had always taken her hunting with him and she could hit any animal, any time of day, with any weapon. She preferred her musket, but it was hers and recognizable to many of the men who enlisted from Bainbridge. Plus, Josiah knew the gun, how she held it, and how she shot. He knew everything about her, except that she enlisted to be close to him. She admired his bravery and cried as hard as she could when he hugged her one last time before he left. She smelled the fireplace in his jacket, heard him whisper he would always be there for her and would return so they could walk hand in hand down the lane again, and she tasted the sweet cream on his lips from his last dinner in her home. He left her not knowing that she would run off the next morning and enlist farther north after she cut her hair short, saving some to make a mustache, and using her brother's clothes to make her deception complete.

Her brother wouldn't miss them, in fact he would have been honored they served her in battle since his death prevented him from using them himself. She shouldered her father's gun feeling his presence with her as well. He died with his son and wife when a trip upriver turned catastrophic. A huge storm flooded the river and turned their boat over. Everyone traveling on the boat perished, except Etta. She was saved by a floating piece of the mast which carried her to the shore. She was found the next day by Josiah. They never left each other's side. He was going to marry her but news of the war came. He promised if she waited that he would be with her every day for the rest of their lives. Time became her enemy, the South became her enemy, and death became her enemy. They only way she knew she would survive was to ensure Josiah's survival. Even if she died, his life would be worth her death a million times over. So she enlisted and made sure she was always behind him on the front lines... his guardian angel ever present but unbeknownst to him.

She had saved his life two times already by taking out Rebs when they got too close to him. She made out the frame of the soldier as he lifted his gun and took aim. Her shot always rang first and Josiah never knew his death was postponed. He kept fighting and Etta reloaded.

It was mass chaos after Pickett sent his men charging in. The rocky terrain, the stench of decaying bodies, and the mass exhaustion faltered the center of the Union troops where Josiah was. He looked up just as his commander was shot once cleanly through the head and then fell inches away from Josiah's boots. Josiah listened to the man breathe his final two breaths and watched as his eyes closed half way and a stream of blood slid from his mouth to the ground. Josiah felt like his time was nearing its end and saw many of his brother soldiers stand up ready to fight with their bare hands to keep hold of the territory on the hill. That's when the Reb jumped from behind the rock and pointed his musket straight at Josiah's chest. Josiah closed his eyes and waited for the report of the musket, but instead he heard a shot from behind him and saw the man collapse upon himself onto the ground. Josiah's breath caught itself and as he tried to turn around to see where the saving shot came from, he fell. The ball from the musket that killed his attacker rebounded off the rock and lodged itself deep into the top of Josiah's chest. His hand found the wound and the warmth flowing from it. As he fell, he felt arms wrap around his waist. He never hit the ground. Instead, he looked up into the eyes of someone he knew.

"Etta? How are you here? Am I dreaming? Are we home? There was a war..." His coughs interrupted his explanation. "You can't be here Etta. You are home. I'm going to love you forever and we are going to..."

The coughs became more violent and tears began to escape Josiah's eyes. The sounds of guns, cannons, and men fighting were like crickets compared to Josiah's wrenching coughs and gasps. Etta couldn't speak. She just held his head. She was crying too.

"You shot him Etta. You saved me. You never did hit that bear by the cave. You almost shot yourself when that bullet came back at your head." This time his cough was a laugh which made him smile showing the blood filling his mouth. "I think I'll be okay now Etta. We can go home. I feel light. I can see the sun, and I'm tired. Can I rest now Etta?"

His eyes searched hers as she blinked tears which fell onto his forehead. "Yes Josiah. You can rest now. I'll meet you in the lane. Hold out your hand to me and we'll walk all the way to heaven together."

"Etta... my angel Etta... you were always with me..."

Etta watched the life leave his eyes and she took her hat off to place it over his face. The battle continued around her and she saw for the first time how many dead soldiers there were here in Gettysburg. "So many dead..." she thought to herself as she looked at the grey clouds overhead. "Is there ever sunshine during a war?"

She didn't hear the musket or see the shot that hit her. She only heard Josiah whispering her name as a hand reached for her through the sunlight.

10.
Country Life
Deborah Guzzi

The night descends with a button down moon
against a powder blue comforter sky,
fluffed and puffed with goose down feathers
as the cat-and-nine tails burst with seed pride.

Country mothers have called the dinnertime
belled and sent the scent of soup on the wind,
the sneaker pile begins at the backdoor,
even the dog knows, it time to come in.

The kitchen table once set is abandoned
for the folding trays by the big screen TV,
and autumn gourds with gold chrysanthemums
host center stage in the tables display.

Soon, silhouettes will shadow the den walls
and the younger children will rush to bed,
for they hear the call of wild coyote; they run
quickly diving beneath their warm bedspreads.

The families lights dim, as they hideout
and silver starlight covers their ceiling;
Mom has placed plastic stars of Moon and Mars
to usher in good dreams, as they're drifting.

Oh, the nighttime warmth will not last too long
for temperatures drop till dawn arrives,
and the dawn will start with a roosters crow;
yes, the country's the place to be alive!

11.
Coyote Owns the World
Tristan Tavis Marajh

All I do is walk around by myself, nose down and minding my own business. I avoid facing off with you. You might think this is a gesture of deference, but here's a secret: it's repulsion. Yes; disgust. Yet I'm the nuisance, you believe. I'm the sly devil, trickster, the Wiley E., lock-up-your-daughters Coyote. Me. Not Raccoon, with the robber's mask and crazy grin on his face; spilling your organic bins and spreading the mess for you to behold in the morning. Not Moose, standing in your way on the roads, big dopey grin on his face, threatening both your lives should your car collide with his backside. The few coyholes down south that attacked you gave us all a bad name. I've never attacked a human.

But you attacked me. I'm the trickster, you say, yet you tricked me. You snared me, beat and branded me, shoved me in a cage to tear off my hair. For winter fashion. But I escaped. You have not, nor do you seem to want to. You are threading dark and murky waters, humans; a selfish ecosystem. This is your world. Money taints the air around you like a sick fog; stifling your spirits, making you spineless. And yet, you say, you need it to survive. Survive?! Most of you don't know what true survival is. Among you I have seen every demented offspring of fear. I saw how those portions of Earth you call nations are formed and how you let it dictate your emotions and desires. I saw how some of you will die or kill for it, thinking it's the best damn place in the world. I trot across those borders yet you have to stand in long lines of mistrust; remove your shoes and belts then stand in another line to show fellow humans little dark-blue pocketbooks that say nothing about your personality.

And your faiths. They are responses, rebuttals, retorts to the one preceding it. What playthings you all are, for the confused deity you created. But no; I'm the one who can't be trusted. Not Squirrel, who scratches your ceilings and leaves half-eaten apples on your windowsills. Not Skunk either, who has no qualms about dousing you with the fragrance of sweat-sock extract.

Your fellow fellows have it right. Those who were pushed out and corralled. One Life; one and the same with the Earth. But still, you separate yourself. You believe that you are top of the food chain, oh omnivorous apex predators, yet those beneath you get the last laugh – or burp. Those you don't see. You – and the animals you consume – your eyes will all bulge out in terror like a fish's, as you suffocate without the quiet exhalations of trees and grass. Worms will burrow through your rotting corpse. And more trees and weeds will rise and flourish upon you, triumphant. And still you say: you are on top of the food chain! Ha ha! Fool chain, maybe!

12.
Deviled Eggs
Mark Hudson

My grandma's eggs were possessed,
the children refused to ingest.
My niece said the eggs were "gooey.'
and maybe a little bit chewy.
They kept offering them to me,
I ate a whole lot, they were free.
She also made some sloppy Joes,
I finished the meal with some job.
Then the kids wished to play tag,
my stomach was starting to sag.
I chased my nephew and niece,
it was hard, I am quite obese.
Without a sense of humor, I'd cry,
but I had no room left for some pie!

13.
Done
Tyler Lentz

My body is a piece of art
Created by these hopes and dreams
I have a tattoo on my heart
My feelings bursting at the seams
I am the one without a name
And no one even seems to care
My situation stays the same
No one ever said that life was fair

Here in the rain or the snow
Only the weather seems to change
My true feelings will never show
All I can do is re-arrange
With what I see and what I feel
Staying clear and keeping focus
Whatever needed to seem real
In the end, it all seems hopeless

I saw you, you did not see me
Acting like this is something new
I sang to you a melody
All the words that I spoke were true
But the words just passed by your ear
You did not hear a word I said
And in my eye began a tear
Deep inside my sadness has spread

I became someone I am not
Something dark when among the light
And for that I deserve to rot
Sick and twisted and full of spite
The fear set free, beyond control
When I get scared I turn and run
Trying to heal my tortured soul
Now it is over with, I am done

14.
Drowning Man
John Grey

Don't drown.
Reach out.
Damn the madness of the water.
Its tortured swirl.
That crumbling wall of oxygen
above your head.

Hoist yourself up and out of death
and back into the scenic posters:
dunes and cliffs
and beauties sunning.
Bob like a buoy.
Float like paper.
If only you could swim.
Breath, salt, memory, ocean...
what a collage,
what a jumble.

Life.
It's not just theirs.
Not the stick people running
along the distant shore.
Not the ones in the windows
of the seaside cottages.
Don't condemn yourself
to the silt and sludge,
the fish-like trowel
of the unwitting bottom feeder.

Get back into the world.
Any way you can.
Raise yourself up
on your chill, your wetness.
Grip your fear, your panic.
and don't let go.
Be who you've yet to be.
Not a lung-less monument
to the years you've lived.
Cry out. Go on.
Hear yourself
so you'll know it's you.

15.
Dust Motes
Jane Riley Peterson

It is the sprinkles of dust
        that is our love
   To cover the plant leaves
        is the taste
To cover the table cloth is the distant relation
Remote is the taste of leaves on cloth

16.
Founding Fathers
Chase Pielak

You never hear the best part of independence:

For a year –
Or maybe two,
During the deafening roar,

A tiny little life clings
To you
Silhouetted in blinked lightning

This Fourth of July,
I'll remember forever:

Every firework
Holding me for dear life.

This, perhaps, they felt too.

17.
Fugue
Chase Pielak

Underneath a crow's commentary
answer echoed off the façade:
time hangs suspended – gliding – immobile

through the unseasonably sunned sky.
Together we speculate
about whether it's possible

to find harmony.
She (who I don't know) – is singing softly
on the patio corner

about heart-break.
I can't sing.
All I can do is write.

18.
Glacial Point
A.J. Huffman

Blizzard.
Opaque blanket.
Coat's billowing powder,
dusting, shimmering.   A frosting,
endured.

19.
Grandmother's Dress
Valerie J. Winston

This story was inspired by a former student who lost her grandmother and wore an altered dress of hers to give the valedictory dress at her high school graduation. It was also inspired by my special closeness to my own grandmother.

It is a beautiful June day. The sun is shining, there are a few wispy clouds, and a slight breeze is gently blowing. There is no sign of rain on this perfect wedding day. My granddaughter is getting married to her special love. He is a wonderful young man and will surely make her happy.

I smile as I remember her giddy excitement when she got engaged. I thought she would pass out from pure joy. I remember that same rush of excitement when I got engaged. From that point on everything became a whirlwind of excitement.

My smile begins to fade as I feel a twinge of regret and disappointment. I love my granddaughter dearly and thought she truly understood about the dress, but I discovered that I was wrong. She decided on a dress from a fancy bridal salon. What made it so disheartening was that she couldn't seem to tell me herself. She let her mother break the bad news. Maybe my granddaughter and I weren't as connected as I thought and hoped we were. In any case, I have decided to let it go. This is her special day and I'll not ruin it by dwelling on the past or on the dress.

My thoughts are interrupted as music begins to play. The procession will begin shortly. As I look around at the beautiful flowers and the surrounding gardens I can't help but think of the dress once more and how perfect it would have looked in this setting. It was made for a place such as this. I sigh heavily as I decide again that I must let it go. But try as I might I can't help it as the procession begins and my mind drifts back to the first time I saw the dress.

****

It was the beginning of my senior year in high school and I was in one of my typical teenage moods.   However, this was one of my worst ones.   I was so angry.   I was already mad that my parents moved my grandmother in with us.   She was getting too old to stay in her own home and no one was able to afford an assisted living facility.   Instead, they moved her into my room.

For some reason they also decided it would be a good idea for me to be responsible for this grandmother that I barely remembered or knew anything about.   How dare they?   How could they do this to me?   It was bad enough to lose my privacy, but it was my senior year.   Having to look after my grandmother was going to cut into my social life.   Not that I had much of one, but I did like to have my own time and my own space.   To say that I was resentful would have been a gross understatement.

And being the horrible teenager that I was, I became sullen and rude to my grandmother.   I would make snide remarks and comments or just ignore her completely.   My grandmother seemed to take my behavior all in stride, however.   She never got upset, at least that I saw.   And then one day I got a rude awakening.

My grandmother would sometimes talk to herself or this old picture she carried around all the time.   She never showed it to me, or anyone else for that matter, and I never asked to see it.   I didn't even really pay attention to what she was saying.   One night, after returning home from a football game, I heard my grandmother talking as I came up the stairs.   For some reason I decided to listen and stood in the hallway just outside my bedroom door.

I realized she was talking to my late grandfather and that it must be his picture she carried around.   I'd never met this grandfather.   I was shocked when I heard my name and discovered she was telling him all about me.   What was more shocking was how complimentary she was being.   She talked about holding me as a baby and how much she missed being able to watch me grow up.   She said that she knew I would turn out to be beautiful.   She also told him that I was smart and talented, and would go on to do great things.

I couldn't believe it.   How was she able to see so much in me when I couldn't even see it myself?   And how was it she could speak so pleasantly about me when I had been nothing but rude to her?   I felt tears begin to sting my eyes as I began to feel so horrible for the way I had been acting and how I had treated my grandmother.   No matter what I said or how I'd behaved, she loved me.   Even though we didn't really know one another that well, she still loved me.   In that moment I began to understand what unconditional love meant.

I slowly walked into the room, intending to apologize.   The look on my grandmother's face told me that she knew I'd been listening.   I started to say something, but words failed when I noticed what my grandmother was wearing.   It was the most beautiful dress I'd ever seen.   We stared at one another for a moment, speechless.   I could see the moisture building in her eyes and I know that she saw the same in mine.   She slowly raised her arms and reached out to me.   I rushed into those open arms and began to sob like a baby.

All the anger that I'd been feeling was released in those tears and in that hug.   My grandmother held me with a strength I didn't know she had.   I felt her love in those strong arms.   We held each other for a long time.

****

I am distracted from the past as the ushers arrive to put the runner in place.   They struggle a bit in getting it down the aisle.   It won't be long now before my own granddaughter makes her appearance. I let the memories wash over me again.

****

That night things changed between me and my grandmother. The dress she was wearing that night had been her own wedding dress. She told me that whenever she was truly missing my grandfather she would put it on and remember how special their time together had been. The dress itself was tea length with a form-fitting bodice, and a skirt that flared slightly from the waist. The skirt was made up of three layers with some tulle and lace. The neck was scooped and had a cutout peephole that accentuated my grandmother's graceful neck. It was finished off with cap sleeves. But the most beautiful part of the dress was the print. It was a floral print with purple flowers throughout. It looked like a watercolor painting.

That same night, my grandmother told me her wonderful love story and I learned just how special this dress was and why it meant so much to her. My grandparents met when they were only eight years old. Both families worked as sharecroppers on an old plantation in Mississippi. From the moment they met they were inseparable. As they grew up, they grew in their love for one another.

My grandfather knew that he wanted to marry my grandmother, but he wasn't making enough money as a sharecropper to provide a good home and a good life for the both of them. So he decided to move North for a while to get a better job and earn more money. He promised to return to her. It took many years of hard work for them both.

During those years apart my grandmother began to prepare for her wedding. She searched for the perfect dress that would express all that she was feeling about the love they shared. The dress would signal the beginning of their beautiful life together.

But she couldn't find one that suited her or at a price she could afford. It was her own grandmother that stepped in to help her. They began to collect scraps of fabric and requested cast-offs from dress and fabric stores. They asked friends and neighbors to help out when they would travel out of town.

After a while, there was enough fabric to begin work on the dress. They hand-painted the purple flowers and then carefully sewed all the pieces together. By the time her love returned, the dress was complete. What was once scraps had truly become a work of art under the guiding hands of her grandmother. The two women carefully picked flowers for her bouquet that would match the dress. The wedding took place in a fragrant, blooming garden in the month of June.

****

I was pulled from my memories once again at the sound of laughter. The flower girl was putting on quite a show as she very deliberately dropped each petal. I noticed that there were mostly purple petals mixed in with a few other colors. They looked to be almost the same color as in the dress, that dress, my grandmother's dress. I'm kidding myself if I'm thinking that I can forget about that dress on this day of all days. I think back to when I actually took possession of the dress.

****

I found even greater respect for my grandmother after hearing the story of the dress. I wished that I had been able to know my grandfather. And I one day hoped to have a love as great as theirs had been. I spent more and more time with my grandmother and we became extremely close. I would often ask her to retell the story of the dress.

My senior year flew by and it was soon time for my prom. I had been asked by one or two guys, but didn't think I would be able to go. My parents just couldn't afford it. I could get by without having to buy some things, but I would definitely need a new dress. However, our budget just wouldn't allow it. I worked a few jobs here and there, but I was trying to save that money for college. I eventually gave up on the idea of going.

About a week before the prom took place I came home from school to find my grandmother's dress laying on my bed and she was sitting next to it. She took my hands and told me that she wanted me to wear it to my prom. I started to protest, but saw that this was something she truly wanted me to do. We were both very emotional as I tried on the dress. It fit perfectly. I promised my grandmother that I would be very careful with her dress. I had a great time and received so many compliments on the dress. I shared each wonderful moment with her when I returned home.

The dress was once again packed away and I wouldn't see it again until a few years later when my grandmother passed away. She left specific instructions that I was to be given the dress. She knew that I understood how much the dress meant to her. She knew that I could see all the true beauty in it. She knew that I understood the emotions that went into making it so special. She wanted me to share all of that with my own daughter and pass the dress on.

That would have been a wonderful idea had I not been blessed with three strapping boys. But, I was eventually able to share the story and the dress with my granddaughter. She became curious about the dress after seeing some of my prom pictures. I shared the story of the dress with her and she seemed to understand it. I even offered it to her for her own prom, but she was very hesitant and afraid it would get damaged as she didn't trust some of her fellow classmates not to ruin it. But whenever she would come over she would ask to hear the story and loved to try the dress on from time to time.

And even though I thought she understood the significance of the dress, it hasn't been worn for an event since my own wedding. I, too, was married in the month of June, and in a garden and I wore the dress. I so hoped to see it worn one last time, but that is not to be. I will have to take it out of storage tonight just to see it again. And then I must decide what to do with it. I am not sure if my granddaughter would pass it on should I decide to give it to her. And I don't want it to just end up in a resale store somewhere.

I have yet to see my granddaughter's wedding dress. I think she knew that I would be a bit disappointed with whatever choice she made. But I've relived the life of this dress long enough. I shall endeavor to finally let go of the past and be happy with what she did choose.

****

It is now time to face the music as I hear the "Trumpet Voluntary" begin. It is time for the bride to make her appearance. I brace myself as I stand. I take a deep breath and turn with everyone else to await my granddaughter's entrance. As soon as I see her tears spring to my eyes. She is wearing the dress, my grandmother's dress, my dress, and now her dress. She looks as beautiful as my grandmother did when I first saw her in it, so long ago. She is an absolute vision as she floats down the aisle. I give up trying to maintain my composure as I see she has also recreated the bouquet that both I and my grandmother carried. I am so stunned and surprised.

My granddaughter stops her procession once she gets to me. She hugs and kisses me and whispers in my ear that she loves me and will always cherish this dress. I watch her through teary eyes as she continues her journey to her true love. It has come full circle, this beautiful, water-colored dress, my grandmother's dress.

20.
Grumpy's Testimony
Diana Kathryn Plopa

From the Desk of Max Ink, Daily News Court Reporter
June 14: Far Away Enchanted Kingdom
Circuit Court Part Three

The bailiff takes his place at the front of the room and brings the people to order. "All rise. Court is now in session. The honorable Judge Fairness presiding."

The judge bangs his gavel. "Take your seats, please." He acknowledges the defendant and the plaintiff sitting at their respective tables, and nods to their attorneys. He looks to the defense attorney, "Call your first witness."

"Mr. Snide, counsel for the defense, Queen Anais, your honor. On this third day of due process, we call Mr. Grumpy Dwarf to the stand."

Mr. Grumpy Dwarf shuffles up to the witness box, his hat in his hand, and a scowl on his face.

Mr. Snide sidles up to the witness box, the pants of his perfectly tailored suit holding their creases perfectly as he walked. "Now, Mr. Dwarf..." begins Mr. Snide.

"The name's Grumpy, if ya don't mind." he says with a grumble and a sneer.

"Yes, certainly. Grumpy; as you've already been sworn in, please tell the court, in your own words, what transpired during the week in question."

"Trainspired?" says Grumpy.

"Yes," says Snide. What happened?"

"Ah… you gots some fancy words, don't ya, mister? Well, I suppose it started off as any other regular week. Me an' the boys were headin' off to the mines to dig for stuff like we always do. And when we come back, this… this hussy was in our house! Down right rude, if ya ask me."

"Is the woman you speak of in in the courtroom today?" asks Snide.

"Yes sir. She's sitting right there." Grumpy points his stubby left thumb at Snow White, sitting at the plaintiff's table. He points with his thumb, because he lost the first two fingers of that hand some years ago in a mining accident. It's only part of the reason for his sullied mood; but that's another story.

"If it pleases the court, let the record reflect that Grumpy Dwarf has indicated Ms. Snow White. Go on, Grumpy. Continue with your account."

"I ain't givin' ya no money, mister!" roils Grumpy.

"No, sir, not money… your account… your story of what happened that week," corrects Mr. Snide. He waggles his head in disbelief and not quite loud enough for the jury to hear chides, "where did they find this guy? He's a moron!"

"Well, like I said, we was headin' back from the mines, all hungry an' such, just looking for a little dinner an' rest, when that… that… argh!" Grumpy's face turns bright crimson and his beard prickles away from his face, making him look like a startled porcupine.

"Calm down Grumpy, sir. Just tell us what transpired." reminds Mr. Snide.

"Fine," he says, clearing the anger from his throat. "She came into our house, uninvited an' started rummaging around. She moved stuff we didn't want moved... ya know, cobwebs an' such. She washed the dishes that we'd purposefully left in the sink... no need for her to do that, we gots more. An' she MADE THE BEDS, TOO! The gall, I tell ya! An' then, she made us BATHE! I don't know who this harlot thought she was, strutting into our home as if she ran the place. The others... well... they went right along... swayed by a pretty face, they were. But not me. Oh no! I stood my ground. I told 'em, we can't keep her. She's not a puppy, after all. An' for my mind, a heap more trouble! I knew somebody would be missing her an' come for her... an' wreck our lives even more than this one already done did. I reckoned they'd even come for the mine. But did the boys listen to me... NO! They just pranced around the house like Dopey, there... all twitter-pated with stupidity. It was disgraceful."

"Then what happened, Mr. Grumpy?" cajoled Mr. Snide once again.

"Well, it was just as I told 'em... but they didn't want to listen to me, NO! Those ingrates... sometimes I think the lot of 'em is just simply daft. Stark crazy, I tell ya!" Grumpy was working himself up into a genuine froth now... spittle dripping from the corner of his mouth where he lost some control in that past mining accident... but I digress.

Mr. Snide enjoyed the theatrics of his star witness, and egged him further. "Go on, sir... just recount the facts for the court. How did things change for your clan after Snow White entered your lives?"

"Well, as I said, the day of reckoning finally came. She didn't listen to us... let some stranger into the house... and BAM! Next thing we know, she's laying on the floor, near dead. I said good riddance to ya... but the boys... those foolish curs, they were smitten. Brainwashed, I tell ya! They actually wanted to put her in some stupid glass box to keep her forever. We're miners, for crimaney's sake, not taxidermists!   I just don't know what they were thinkin'. The whole thing was like making gold out of a box of rocks, I tell ya!"

"Please continue..." Snide encouraged, eager to capture his audience with the climax of the story.

"Well, that's when it happened," said Grumpy in a voice that was almost a whisper – quite the feat for such a crotchety old man.

Mr. Snide leaned in real close, his voice low and his body tense. "What, Mr. Grumpy, what happened?"

"We had to deal with... with... I can hardly say it..." Grumpy looked away from Snide, toward the townsfolk in the jury box. His face held the shame he knew was real.

"Go ahead," said Mr. Snide. "Take your time... find your words, Mr. Grumpy. What did you have to deal with?" Snide was waiting for the magnificent punchline he knew would sway this case.

"LOVE!" howled Grumpy.

Mr. Snide took a step back, eyed the jury with a heavily loaded pregnant pause, and said, "Love, sir?"

"Yes, LOVE!" bellowed Grumpy. "It's outrageous!   We'd never had to deal with that infernal nonsense before. Our lives were simple... we went to the mine every day, did our work, came home, ate a bit, slept a bit, an' got up the next day to do it all again. We had a good life!   An' then, this... this... wretched female came along an' made us all care for her!   She wrecked everything! Bollixed up the whole works, I tell ya! Now, we had this woman to care for... an' she took her toll on us, I might tell ya! All that washing, an' proper table manners, an' making the beds each morning... It was ridiculous. We had a good life before she came...

an' then she went and complicated it all to pieces!   The nerve of that woman!   The boys an' I actually started CARING. ARGH!   It's enough to drive a person daft, I tell ya!"

Grumpy took a moment to look around the room for some sign that he'd made his point... knowing that surely, there would be others in the courtroom who heard his plight and understood. Blank faces stared back at him. Grumpy went on with his story, hopeful that someone would understand and be on his side.

"An' then, when she was lying there, in that pretty box, sleeping an' such... well, I thought that finally we were rid of her. Finally, we could have our lives back. No more washing... no more cleaning... and no more CARING. But she couldn't leave well enough alone... No! Not this one. No sir!" He thrust his stubby thumb at Snow White again, punctuating his disdain.

Mr. Snide coaxed him again, directing the play with just as much intensity as he thought the judge would allow. "We want to hear your story, Mr. Grumpy. Tell us what happened."

"Well, this fancy pants prince came along and kissed her! Can ya imagine... the unmitigated nerve of the fellow... I mean KISSING a near-dead lady. Have ya ever heard such nonsense!" Grumpy spat his disgust at the prince who sat beside Snow White.

"What happened after the kiss, Mr. Grumpy?" cajoled Snide, again.

"Well, she surprised us all, she did. She sat right up an' kissed him right back. Then she jumped out of her glass box, an' said that we were all going to live with this Mr. Fancy Pants at his castle someplace farther away from the mine. What right did she have to say where we would live? An' we didn't have no say in it, neither. It's just wrong, I tell ya!" Grumpy's face again lit up like Rudolph's red nose, his whiskers alive with static electricity.

"So," interjected Mr. Snide; "she wanted to essentially kidnap you, and take you away from the only home you've ever known? Is that right, sir?" Snide had a cat-ate-the-canary grin on his face. He was proud of his star witness. "Grumpy sure is hitting this one out of the park," he murmured to no one in particular.

"Darn right, that's right! And she ain't got no right! I'm still the only one in charge of me... Ain't nothing gonna change that." Grumpy pounded his fist on the witness box, and looked adamantly at the judge. "It's criminal, I tell ya! Just criminal! She should be in jail or somethin'. It just ain't right!" The judge sat stoic... unaffected by the theatrics.

"Thank you, Mr. Grumpy." said Mr. Snide. "You may step down."

The judge banged his gavel on the desk once again. "Okay folks. We'll take a short recess, and return for cross examination after lunch. Court is adjourned."

21.
Heal Me
Carmanie Bhatti

(Inspired by true story of a physically challenged girl)

I fear to step in
the world of joy, for I am
a marginalized soul

There is no space for
recreation, healing of
my wounds, and deep pains

I want my Christ to
heal me, so that I may walk ,
play sing, dance, rejoice !

22.
Hermits
David Lee
Featherman

So one night last winter these two guys walk into my bar just before last call... Yeah, I know, my friend. Sounds like the opening line from a lousy joke. But just maybe it's the opening to the Twilight Zone. Tell you the god's honest truth? I'm still not sure what to believe, and after twenty years tending bar and swapping stories, I thought I'd heard it all.

Anyway, business is slow that night, what with heavy snowfall for two days straight. We'd had near to three hundred inches—lake-effect off Superior—and it isn't even the end of February; that can wear down even the most die-hard of us Yoopers. So I'm about to cash out early and head upstairs for some shuteye when in walks the first guy lookin' every bit the Troll from somewhere below the Mackinac Bridge. Could ha' been a two thousand-calorie-a-day, thirty-something model from Eddie Bauer's winter clothes and accessories catalogue—except for the butterfly bandage covering what must be a nasty cut just above a beaut of a black eye.

He's unwinding a wooly scarf when in stomps the second guy. He's kinda slouched a bit, but as he's smackin' snow from the brim of his trapper's hat and hookin' a heavily-worn mackinaw on the wall peg I'm guessin' he's a good three or four inches taller than me—I'm six-one, at least I was at Camp Lejeune, back in the day. Barrel-chested—figure he weighs in at near to two-seventy-five. Dressed like a jack—wool red and green checkered shirt, black suspenders holding up ranger-type knickers tucked into knee-high boots. I'm thinkin' he looks more German than Finnish or Norwegian: big boney head; silvery blond hair, thin on top, pulled loosely into a ponytail; and a prominent nose that leaves no doubt he's been in a fight or two over the years. As he's drawing his stool up to the bar, I catch his glance—pale, nearly translucent-blue eyes—reminds me of wolves or coyotes I've shined during deer season—before his eyes dart away to the display of whiskey bottles behind me. His heavy grey stubble's carved by furrows that remind me of the narrow creeks and rivers fanning out from springs in the Porcupine Mountains—up here we call 'em the Porkies—and then keep dividing as they flow through stands of poplar, birch and white pine into Superior. Can't miss 'em along the shoreline within two or so miles either side of this bar. Anyway, I'm guessing the big guy's pushing eighty anyway; a few more miles on 'im than I've clocked.

By now the Troll's also at the bar, a single stool separating my two remaining patrons. The younger guy has one of those well-shined bald heads and sports a heavy beard—no doubt professionally-styled; tells me there's vanity to spare. When he orders, I think I hear 'schnapps on the rocks.' Up here that's a drink more popular with our ladies. And I'm wondering... but I do a heavy pour of our best (and only) peppermint schnapps over rocks. He looks at it, takes a whiff and says, "Excuse me but what is this?"

At which point, without turning toward either of us, the jack—who's not more than nodded since he entered—says, "The man ordered scotch on the rocks," in a voice heavy with gravel. Then he points to a bottle at the furthest end of my shelf; "See that one malt scotch there—label says it's Sheep Dip," and I sorta chuckle to myself. He nods toward the Troll and says: 'Pour 'im some over cubes, then set me up with three shots. On second thought just leave the bottle; I'll pour. Bring a glass for you,' and then he's rollin' up his sleeves. Like as I said, he's a burly guy, so when he crosses forearms on the bar, his veins nearly pop.

Now I'm thinkin', he looks vaguely familiar. On the other hand, he's dressed and talks every bit like a lot of us Yoopers: maybe down on his luck but no doubt struggling to make the best of it, what with the economy in the toilet—mines shut down; paper mill sold for scrap. Hell, those corporate bastards in Tennessee even tore up our only railroad tracks and sold them too, would you believe? Anyway, 'scruffy with pride', yessir, that's how I think of us Yoopers. But there's somethin' about this guy I can't yet put my finger on. Shoot, Hollywood might cast him as the quintessential mountain man. Got the eagle eyes of one, too. I'm wondering how the heck he read that Sheep Dip label—it's a good eight or nine feet from his stool. I can barely read it, and I'm wearin' glasses for everything at my age—well, nearly everything.

So I say, "outstanding choice, Mister." And as I'm doin' the set ups I tell him my brother-in-law from the Lower Peninsula flies up with a case each deer season. Floated me a loan to buy this bar when I retired from the pulp mill. He's captain for an international airline and gets to fly fish in England and Scotland. This so-called one malt scotch is something of a joke, he once told me. The old timer sheep farmers near his favorite stream in England used to call whiskey 'sheep dip,' and so some upstart distillery decided to slap that on its bottles for local distribution. As my brother-in-law says, "It's not as smooth as silk pantaloons on a French whore's ass, but its kick is every bit as enjoyable."

Well, up to now the Troll's been silent—taking it all in, I guess, although at first I'm thinkin' he looks just a bit dazed. As Mountain Man pours, the other guy finally pipes up. "Thanks for the drink, Mister. Carson, Gil Carson," he says and extends his hand. The big guy continues his pours, gives a low grunt and shallow nod in Carson's direction, but doesn't introduce himself. So I reach for Carson's hand across the bar, "People just call me Stubb," I tell him and ask what brings him to Union City. "Looks like you might've had a bit of trouble along the way," I say, motioning toward the wounds on his forehead and eye.

"I'm a photojournalist, a freelancer working an assignment for a tourism magazine in Chicago," he says. Tells us he's to write a story 'bout the unprecedented ice that's closing just about all of Lake Superior that winter and shoot photos inside the walk-in caves they'd heard about down Illinois way.

"Some of my customers seen 'em," I tell him. "Drove snow machines way out or snowshoed into coves usually unreachable except by fishing boat or kayak in summers; spectacular, they say, caves created underneath enormous, high waves that look flash frozen in motion, like as time got stopped by the bitter cold." I tell 'im maybe his story'll send more of the tourist trade our way. That's about all we have up here anymore, my friend.

At that, Mountain Man hurrumphs and tosses in a quick, "Sure 'nough, that's all we need: more tourists trompin' through the woods," but keeps staring at the shot in his fist.

Anyways, the journalist had planned to fly to Marquette or Ironwood but flights up here were cancelled because of those Alberta Clippers over the prior weeks, so he rents a car and heads toward Union City as a first stop, he says. I ask if he's ever driven up here in winter; no, he says, but he'd rented a four-wheel drive, had GPS on his iPhone, and packed some survival gear. I'm thinking: out of an Eddie Bauer catalog, no doubt.

Mountain Man's pouring second shots by this point. The further north the journalist gets from the Wisconsin line into the U.P., the squall line's spinnin' near constant white out. On top of that, it's real dark, even though not yet six o'clock. He says, "And I'm really in the boonies." Well, I'm not surprised when he also says his iPhone quits working. Cell towers up here are still few and far between, especially closer to the Porkies. And so without GPS he gets turned around on unfamiliar secondary roads, and soon enough he pitches off what he thinks is the roadway, nose down into the ditch. "Banged my head against something before the airbag explodes," he says. Takes him a while to gather his senses after that; maybe he's knocked out for a bit, but he can't say for sure. "I suddenly realize the airbag's pinning me to the seat, and I start to panic," he says. So he fishes for the Swiss Army knife he always carries—mostly uses it to open wine at picnics, I'm thinking. Luckily, he can climb out of his car through the back hatch. Sees blood on his jacket; he touches his forehead and figures his splitting headache could be more than just that. Somehow he applies a butterfly patch from the first aid kit in his gear. He'd practiced putting on showshoes before the trip, he says, but in pitch darkness and blowing snow they keep crossing as he's side-steppin' up the embankment with a flashlight and a couple flares. As he's lighting the flares, he thinks he smells the faint aroma of wood smoke but can't tell from which direction. His adrenalin starts pumping, he says, and the panic's easing up. So he sidesteps down to his car, throws on a small backpack with the survival gear, and locks up, 'cause he's leavin' his camera stuff and all.

Now this is where the journalist's story gets real interesting. He's standing on the road—in about a foot of new, drifting snow by then—and he's castin' his flashlight from side-to-side and doin' a three-sixty-degree shuffle: Where's that smell of wood smoke coming from? All of a sudden his light beam catches a flash, but he's not too sure since it's still blowing snow in his face. So he retraces his arc, and sure enough, there it is again: two sets of eyes in the brush, about twenty or so feet ahead he guesses. And he thinks the smoke might be coming from that direction, too. More adrenalin, he says. He shuffles ahead slowly; he's still dizzy. He lowers his beam making sure his boots are secure in the 'shoes, and when he looks up again the eyes are gone. And then it hits him: Suppose it's a wolf or worse, a bear and her cub? 'Course, this city guy don't know it's too early for new cubs to be out and about and not likely momma bear, and a black bear at that. Anyway, just then wouldn't you know, the eyes are back, and now they're dead ahead—maybe ten feet—but just one set of 'em in the middle of the road. He exhales 'cause the beam catches the outline of the animal: it's not shaped like bear and too small for wolf—coyote, at least that's what he guesses, 'tho up here they're hard to tell from a

German Shepherd. He's no sooner made his bet with fate, he says, than his coyote turns tail and fast trots away. But not far—maybe twenty, thirty feet—and then heads into the brush, only to peer out and then trot a few feet closer onto the road. Then the guy adds this interesting tidbit: "As I shine my beam on him, he looks away— avoiding the light probably, but I'm wondering: Is he signaling me to follow? And then I notice his limp as he retreats again: most of the right hind leg is missing."

As the journalist is layin' all this out, Mountain Man's still gripping his shots; can't tell from his face if he's been listening or not. But at the mention of the three-legged coyote his head comes up; I catch him glaring into the mirror behind the bar.

Carson is saying he and the coyote continue their cycle of advance and retreat until the car is maybe a quarter mile behind. Soon the flares will burn out, he figures. "And for some odd reason," he says, "I'm not freaking out." Then as the squall is lettin' up a bit, his beam catches the coyote leap ten or so feet off the roadway and limp into what seems to be a cut; looks like an old logging road when he finally pushes into the brush, but it's partially overgrown with birch and cedar. As best he can, he picks up his pace so as not to lose the animal. "The aroma of smoke is really strong now," he says. Before too long the trail opens into a clearing; although his vision is obscured, he detects the outlines of several buildings, some tall, some squat, but directly ahead is a small cabin. He figures he must've been close to the State Park in the Porkies when he went into the ditch, so maybe this is a remote ranger station. Up closer, he sees it's a steep-roofed split-log shack with smoke streaming from a metal chimney. Its frosted windows are flickering with a dim yellow glow, and even though his heart is pounding in his ears, Carson hears dogs barking their warning inside. The journalist is removing his snowshoes when off behind some cedar trees he hears yipping, then an eerie howl that gives him the shivers when it changes octaves; the barking stops. He mounts a couple rickety steps onto a roofed open porch and knocks.

I glance at Mountain Man: his shoulders are set back, coiled and still glaring at the mirror.   All this while the journalist seems lost in his tale—like he's dictating notes, practicing what he'll write up later for his editor—paying no heed to either Mountain Man or me.

A short, sinewy man, maybe in his mid-to-late sixties, meets him at the door.   Before either of them speaks, the man waves at Carson to enter quickly.   The journalist's immediate thought is he's about to ask for help from a hobbit: at most he's five feet four, wearing a peaked brown felt hat with a floppy brim that nearly covers his wild, bushy eyebrows and tilts slightly to one side and deeply down his grey-haired neck; he's thickly bearded, and while that and a mustache virtually obscure his mouth, it can be located by the corncob pipe gripped in one corner; his arms appear somewhat too long, but perhaps due to the cuffs of his faded red wool shirt ending above his wrists; and his bibbed stained overalls would have covered his feet except for well-worn, heavy-soled working boots. Standing close to him, Carson says, "I can smell animals—horses, maybe even pigs."

The journalist apologizes for intruding and introduces himself, but before he can explain his predicament, the hobbit blurts out, "I'm George," and abruptly shuffles toward the back wall of the tiny main room to steady a ladder. Climbing down, from an open-faced loft—maybe a bedroom—is a second short man. "And this here's my brother, Gustav," he says. "Over at the kitchen table, cleanin' his Mauser, that there's our nephew Hugo." And with that the pipe goes back in place.

Well sir, with that a flash bulb goes off, and I'm thinking: Holy Mary, Joseph and Jesus.   This can't be.   I'll get to that later, my friend.

Anyway, Carson's still laying out the flow of his story: Without skipping a beat, Gus jumps right in after George goes silent, boasting that Hugo shot himself a six-pointer early that morning. "Tracked 'im hisself," the uncle stresses, "along a ridge over by Mud Creek. Boy thought he'd wait for a clean shot in the ear hole but missed low and got bib instead, right Hugo?" Gus is tee-heeing and then yanks the kid's chain a bit: "I keep tellin' yah, son, allow yourself a wider bead with deer, when you're startin' out."

Well, the deer takes off, and Hugo's following the blood trail, 'cause he'd nipped the buck. Must've then crept on its belly behind some brush into a swale. So Hugo circles around and nails 'im as he scrambles out.

Uncle says, "Strung 'im up and gutted 'im out before trudging three miles in deep snow to hitch up the sleigh and fetch the carcass. Had the skin rolled off, tenderloins stripped out, and quartered 'im in no time, Hugo did."

Gus turns to the journalist: "You a hunter?" Carson owns up to never even holding a gun. The uncle titters and says, "Well, I hope you're not one of them vegetarians, 'cause over there's a kettle of venison stew I cooked up after Hugo done the hard work. That's all the eats for tonight."

Now while the uncle's been boastin' about his nephew, Carson's figuring Hugo to be in his mid-teens but gives off an impression of being older: kid's already over six feet. Hair's close cut, military style, and so blond that in the amber lantern light, Carson could swear it glows. When Hugo stands up to stow the rifle, his head almost grazes the kitchen ceiling, 'cause the loft's just above. Walking past Gus, the kid's at least a head taller and much bulkier than either of his hobbit-like uncles.

Carson says from the very start he's struck by an air of confidence about the kid. I won't forget Carson's description: "His stride when he walks—it's not like some nonchalant teenager's— and he carries himself like a fellow who's been tested, who's confident he could take care of himself in the deep woods," because it triggers another flash.

As if he could read my thoughts, Mountain Man pushes back hard so's the stool legs screech like a crazed owl. Without a word, he circles around the bar and takes down another bottle. His back is turned. Carson's quiet; his eyes, like mine, fix on the broad back and bowed head. When the big guy finally faces our way, he's glaring down at the journalist, eyes penetrating as if into his soul, "You say you saw 'em both, do you? The hermit uncles? They talked to you."

Carson nods and shrugs his shoulders, like as that's what happened—so what's the problem?

"And you saw him, too, the kid?" The big guy's challenge sounds even stronger.

Another nod, but Carson's lookin' real puzzled.

Well sir, I'm holding my breath.

Mountain Man breaks his gaze and pours out another round—I notice he serves the journalist first. "Here, drink up," he barks. The bottle comes down hard on the bar. Then he puts those eyes on me; I feel 'em probing, like inside my head, for some long seconds before he says, "Stubb, you best lock up. We'll be at this for a while." I could swear his words ended in a gravelly growl.

For several hours, Mountain Man takes charge of the conversation, asking all sorts of questions. I try to lower the tension and suggest we move to more comfortable chairs around one of the tables, so's we can talk better face to face. Knowing what I think I'm startin' to realize, however, I mostly just want to be quiet and take it all in.

"Okay, Carson," Mountain Man begins, "pick up where you left off."

Carson's by now fidgeting and sipping his whiskey seems like every thirty seconds. Says Gus does most of the talking at the kitchen table, relatin' how he and George volunteered as caretakers some years ago. "Here at the Halliwell Mine," the uncle says and gestures with a thumb toward the back of the shack. "Can't suppose you seen the adit shaft or the engine house for the hoist and pulleys; there's a sawmill, too," he says. "Well, all's shut down just now; owners say it's still too expensive extractin' copper from the calcocyte vein," Gus tells him. But he's certain it'll reopen.

"Did once before," George murmurs as he's relightin' his pipe.

Carson learns the uncles grew up a couple or so miles south, at another mine location or company town called Nonesuch. As Gus tells it, the name refers to a peculiar vein of copper ore unlike any other, not like the native or sheet copper in the Keweenaw mineral range running northeast from the Porkies through Houghton and Hancock. At the Nonesuch their father did bookkeeping for the owners in England. Their mother and the eight brothers and sisters tended a huge garden in summer that once fed as many as three hundred or so miners and family members. Carson says somehow that reminds Gus they need to refill their water barrels, and he tells Hugo he should hitch up the sleigh in the morning and head to the spring on the Little Union. And that more or less ends the tellin' of family history and the sparse but hearty meal.

And then Gus pours what the journalist describes as pretty good wine that he and George ferment from their plum and wild cherry trees. It's now maybe a couple or so hours since he'd knocked on their door, and no one's asked what brought the journalist to their shack. Odd, he'd thought, before volunteering how it happened; odder still that no one seems surprised by his encounter with a three-legged coyote. All the while Carson's doin' his explaining, George is tendin' to various chores—refillin' the kerosene lanterns, stokin' the potbelly heater in the center of the shack with dry wood he fetches from behind the kitchen—and then sits arms crossed, smokin' his corn cob, next to his nephew. Both occasionally stroke a couple dogs at their feet—an old female spaniel and a bigger spaniel or mongrel mix Hugo calls 'Laddie.'

After Carson finishes his story, Hugo dashes into the freezing dark to the two-holer before climbing the ladder to the loft, and George is lighting a hand lantern. Gus says George always checks the barn and their two horses at the end of the day. They'll hitch them up and pull out Carson's car when the storm lets up; he can stay the night in the loft with him and the nephew.

"Describe Gus," Mountain Man interrupts.

Carson allows as he stood even a tad shorter than George but appeared more cleaned up: hair trimmed, slicked down and combed straight back off a balding high forehead. Had a similar broad nose but wore horn rim glasses. They give the journalist an impression of Gus bein' more educated, maybe reads a lot. He'd a thin, clean shaven face, Carson remembers. No strong odors of animals on his clothes—plain wool shirt and pale plaid pants; wore a belt, no suspenders. In his early or mid-sixties; appearances being what they are, he looked younger than George.

Mountain Man interrupts again, with an odd question, seems to me just then. "How'd he walk?" Carson asks what he means. "Did he have a limp?"

"Well, not that I notice at first," Carson says. "But later that night, when we're in the loft, he's sitting on his bed unstrapping a prosthesis from his thigh." Gus must've noticed Carson lookin' curious because he tells the journalist he'd nearly lost the whole right leg from gangrene—whacked his toes clean through a boot splittin' wood a few winters back and didn't get to the hospital some twenty miles away until the infection got real bad.

While Carson's been answering questions, I'm keepin' my

eye on the big guy. A couple times there's just the hint of a nod, at the journalist's description of the two hermits. And his shoulders gradually uncoil. As the journalist finishes about Gus' missing leg and slouches in silence, Mountain Man mouths something like, "So the uncles did let you in," and I'm wondering if he's talking to himself or Carson. He's still got a bead on the journalist, and yet the fierceness has left his eyes.

Momentarily, he speaks up more clearly: "If you still got more in you, Carson, tell me." And then he reaches across the table to pass him what's left in my last bottle of Sheep Dip.

Well after downing a shot and pouring a second, the journalist seems somewhat revived and back into tale-dictating mode. By the by, he says, before daylight anyway, he's roused from the dead by a ruckus beneath the loft. Hears Gus cuss a blue streak. Carson's suddenly conscious of loud pops, like hot sap snapping and smells smoke; on the sloping ceiling just above his face, there's flickers of orange. Shack's on fire, he's sure. He bolts upright, and in what little light there is from lanterns below, makes out glowing hair disappearing down the ladder. The journalist rolls out of his bunk still half asleep, knocks his head against the ceiling—hopping about, pulling his boots on—and catches his balance at the very edge of the loft. He's peering down at George and Gus poised like two prize fighters ready to have a go. George must've been fueling the potbelly when it happened—when Gus tossed his pan of shaving water at his brother, 'cause Carson sees suds 'n all in George's beard, and the top of his union suit is drenched. The pan's upturned at Gus' feet. The open potbelly's a sizzlin'. But before either pugilist could more than waggle fists and jab in space, Hugo's between 'em, towering over both. Has 'em by their shirts: "Settle down, you two. What's going on?" Well, at that, both uncles near to collapse after Hugo releases 'em—in what seems like mutual embarrassment to Carson.

Then Gus builds back a little steam: "Your uncle here got drunk as a skunk last night after the rest of us tucked in. See those empty wine bottles near the rat hole he calls a bedroom?" Carson's still looking down on the scene but follows Gus's finger to a narrow closet-like space, between the kitchen and the potbelly in the open room. "And look see here, on the floor of my kitchen. Must've done that after stoking the fires, crawlin' on his hands and knees to his filthy mattress, spittin' his chaw along the way. Just look at this mess! Must've been when the horse kicked and broke his jaw that all good sense got knocked outta him." Well, George says nary a word, but draws out a pouch from a rear pocket, places a pinch of shredded tobacco inside a cheek, turns, and slinks to his lair.

From his perch in the loft, Carson forms a mental picture of the shack that he couldn't take in earlier. He describes it as the inside of what you might imagine knowing it's home to two old hermits. Certainly shows no signs of a feminine touch, like curtains or table cloths or rugs on the floor. What strikes the journalist's eye—remember he's a photographer, too—is that the whole inside could fit into one frame, maybe need a wide-angle lens. And that's just it, Carson says, everything in the frame looks like it's been in place for a very long time, like he's looking at a photograph. There's dust everywhere, so when the places were set out for dinner, Gus had to wipe scraps of food and grime off the rough wood table. Piles of newspapers and magazines, goin' back who knows to when, are here and there, especially near the corner where the kitchen galley and the open room meet—by George's lair. Stacks of shot guns and rifles—maybe a dozen or more stand as if on guard in a couple other corners, and Carson sees boxes upon boxes of cartridges and shells arranged helter-skelter along a shelf above a pile of dry firewood near the potbelly. Kettles, pans and dishes in the kitchen galley lack the likes of cupboards, and so the sink, without plumbing of any sort, is their refuge. And aside from four or five wooden chairs that arrange around the kitchen table or around the potbelly, there's nothin' to suggest it's a place to rest a spell. Not even the steeply-sloped loft offers much comfort, arranged as a bunkhouse but with two metal double bed frames and thin mattresses on springs that each sleep two men, if there's a visitor like Carson or a jack down on his luck. He finishes his description this way: "And then there's the near constant dim light from the kerosene lamps, lending a yellowish-tint to the image, like a sepia photograph."

Well, Carson picks up the story again, sayin' before long it's near to daylight and George is out to the horses, feeding chickens, and gathering eggs. The shack smells of pan frying fish—Gus tells 'im over breakfast these are what's left of last season's smelt, frozen in ice blocks and kept beneath sawdust in the fruit cellar— and of the yeasty aroma of Gus' sourdough bread. Says he's been cookin' at lumber camps and mine locations most of his adult life.

Pretty soon Hugo says he'll hitch the smaller draft horse and be off to the spring. He flashes his uncle one of those glances—you know, what teenagers do when they'd rather do the thing by themselves or in their own way—when Gus tells 'im to take Carson along.

Now the journalist's nearly convinced they've forgotten about his car in the ditch. But he's thinkin' maybe he doesn't need to get to it right away. And he's been gettin' great material for his story, even without his camera.

Well, the storm has blown south of the mountains by mid-morning and they're makin' way along a trail passing through a tunnel of snow-bent cedars. Progress is slow. The draft horse's hooves plod steadily but sometimes the mare is chest-deep in powder. And the runners of the sleigh are fashioned from narrow birch limbs rather than thinner metal rails. Hugo says his uncles were given a beat up sleigh some summers back in trade for venison loins—by a park ranger. Same guy sometimes would appear at his uncles' shack about suppertime—way outta deer season—askin' if they had "any of that fifty cent beef on the stove." His uncles never had a run-in with the rangers, except one, Hugo says. George was drivin' the wagon team back from Union City one hot summer evening after fetching supplies. Hugo volunteers, "My uncles always keep a rifle or shot gun under the wagon seat, so they can pick off grouse." Well, on that occasion, George had bagged about a dozen birds and is just crossin' Mud Creek near sundown when out pops a warden. Asks George what he's got in the bag in the back, because he's still holdin' the shot gun across his lap. Well, he lost the bag and nearly the gun, but a few days later the warden shows up at the shack and tells the uncles that they sure do raise tasty chickens. No trouble since, Hugo says.

The journalist senses a change in Hugo's mood and decides to keep the kid talking, if he can. "So do you live permanently with your uncles?" he starts out. Hugo says he does during summers and on and off in winter, and then goes silent again, 'cept for giddy-uppin' the mare on a steep section. Then the kid just out and says, "They let me do pretty much what I want at the Hell Well," to which Carson responds, "You mean at the shack, at the Halliwell?" Hugo says yes, but it's how he thinks of the place. During Prohibition, so he'd heard, some of the so-called town fathers from Union City used to refer to it as the Hell Well, kinda like an insider's code name. Seems that the hermits once fermented more than fruit wine. Their still was well hidden in the woods, the kid says, and their high-quality 'shine was a well-guarded secret among the local authorities, who were frequent "guests" at the Hell Well. "Still's not far from the spring," Hugo says, "Once we've loaded up, I'll show you what's left. Hikers found it when the Park opened trails nearby."

Their pace is slower returnin' with a partially-filled fifty-five gallon barrel sloshin' in the rear of the sleigh, and the journalist figures he's got time to dig into more personal stuff. "Sounds to me like your uncles have more or less adopted you and given you pretty loose rein," he says, to which Hugo don't reply at first.

"Maybe so," he then offers, "but up here in the mountains you can get yourself lost, injured or killed pretty fast, especially this time of year." Hugo goes on that he's been comin' to the Hell Well since he was about eleven or twelve, first with another uncle, a brother to Gus and George, but lately, he hitches a ride at the pulp mill in Ontonagon with truckers heading back to lumber camps by way of Union City. He usually calls his mom or an aunt from the gas station so they don't worry. From the lake shore there he hikes upstream the last five or so miles along the Union River and crosses to creeks he knows from section maps will lead closer to the shack; and he always carries a compass.

"For my fifteen birthday, Gus and George gave me a 22 pistol," he says, pattin' his long mackinaw. Carson's about to ask if Hugo's parents approve, but the kid continues. "Gus taught me how to shoot, 'cause George has real bad eyes; he can't read or scribble more than his name neither. Pistol's always with me in the woods, for signaling, not hunting—except maybe a rabbit or grouse to eat in an emergency or to scare off a black bear." Says when he's out alone fishing or hunting and the uncles are searchin' for 'im, they fire twice, and if he's in hearing range, he fires back once. And they continue that until they meet up.

But before the uncles allowed him in the woods alone, Gus'd walked him dozens of miles along rivers and streams, high into the Porkies and then down the escarpment to Big Carp Lake and around to smaller spring-fed ponds surrounded by two-hundred-year-old virgin white pine forests. They're deep within the Porkies that few know let alone venture into, the kid says. "I learned how to fish to survive, if necessary, and not just to track and hunt. One day we're fishing for trout along a tributary to the Little Union, near Big Carp Lake," he recounts. "The mosquitoes and black flies are fierce and the banks are tangles of tag alders so we couldn't really cast into the quieter pools under the banks where the trout like to hide." So the uncle tells Hugo to back away quietly and work through the brush downstream just a bit and then set his baited line in waitin' while he goes upstream. "Before long I see tiny rafts of twigs and leaves heading toward me and sure enough, the disturbed trout are out of their hole and swimming my way," Hugo tells the journalist and allows as they stuffed themselves with fresh rainbow after hiking the five or so miles through the brush to the shack.

Carson's still narratin' his trip with Hugo when I catch a glimpse of Mountain Man lowering his head. His eyelids are shut but I can't imagine he's asleep, 'cause he's cupping both empty shot glasses and slowly massaging their lips with calloused thumbs.

So the journalist is sayin' that he and Hugo are maybe a mile from the shack when onto the trail, maybe a hundred yards ahead, bound a doe and a couple young 'uns. They no sooner dash into the brush further along on the opposite side when a couple coyotes burst from the woods in pursuit. The kid says nothin' and Carson's not sure he even took notice, so he lets it drop. But it gets Carson thinking about the three-legged coyote and his car in the ditch.

He says to Hugo, "You know, your uncles showed no surprise when I knocked on your door, and they didn't press to know who I was or what I wanted. Sounds creepy, I know, but it's almost like they already knew."

Well, the kid's silent at first, but Carson surmises that's because they've gotten to a swale and the sleigh's tipping a bit: Hugo's workin' the reins and talkin' to the mare. Eventually he replies, "Folks show up unexpected a lot. Was a guy off a fishing boat two summers ago: lost his brother in a sudden storm when the boat and all their gear sank. He was wearing a preserver and got picked up by another crew. But he lost all he had. Somehow he showed up at the Hell Well, and my uncles took him in; he lived with us into the fall."

Hugo goes on to say that's just about the time a car load of drunks got stuck in deep mud comin' up the mountain from Union City. About two in the morning, Gus, Hugo and the fisherman are asleep in the loft and George is just tucking into his crawl space when two of the drunks pound on the door, bellowing all get out. The dogs are goin' nuts. George is the first one to the door, and when he opens it these clowns tumble inside, laughing themselves silly, as if they were the night's entertainment.

According to Hugo, neither uncle raises his voice. George just trundles to the barn and harnesses up the larger draft horse Rowdy, who Hugo says lives up to his name—it's the one that clobbered George when he was shoeing the big gelding. Hugo and the fisherman take lanterns to find the car, which is easy as the kid tells the story, since the other drunks are singing at the top of their lungs.

Well, they hitch a pair of heavy rusty chains to the car frame. George whispers something into Rowdy's ear, steps away to gather the reins over his high rump and flicks them, gently at first. The horse steps forward 'til the chains are taut. George lets out a 'Heeyahh' and slaps the reins. Rowdy puts all his muscle into it, head down, snorting. There's a sucking sound but the car barely moves. George lets out another 'Heeyahh' and flicks the reins several more times. Now Rowdy's huge hooves are out of the mud and onto gravel; he's scrambling across the stones, iron shoes clattering and sparking until they finally gain steady traction. The car heaves and screeches against rocks onto the roadway. Just then, Gus arrives holding his lantern high so the two weaving drunks in front of him don't tumble into the mud.

Carson tells the kid, "That's a great story; I'll use it in mine." To which the kid replies, "but here's the ending." George unhooks the chains and is leading Rowdy back toward the barn when the drunks pile into the car. Without a word of thanks or even a wave goodbye, they drive off, singing and laughing as if nothing happened. "And you know," Hugo is saying as the sleigh approaches the Halliwell, "I've never heard my uncles say a mean word about those guys. Just like they never complain if some jack down on his luck shows up at their door. Uncle Gus once told me what little any of us has is ours to share."

Then Carson falls silent. He looks to me first and then Mountain Man with that same expression I saw when he walked in—disoriented and dazed. After a minute or so, the big guy raises his eyes off his shot glasses: "And that's all the kid had to say, is that right?" he asks.

"Well, not exactly, but the rest is hazy," Carson admits. Says he keeps trying to piece things together. He can see Hugo standing beside him on a roadway. It's dark. The car's nowhere in sight. Carson's unsure this is where he went into the ditch, but Hugo has no doubt. He still remembers hearing a series of screeching sounds at some distance up the road that winds down the mountains. There's Hugo's voice saying it's the airbrakes of a heavy truck—logs maybe, one like he usually flags down on this stretch, when he figures to go back home. He can visualize a cab light go on as a truck slows—a gasoline tanker—and then the driver reaching toward him as he's about to climb in. He sees himself turn to thank the kid, but he's gone—nowhere in sight. The tanker's brakes hiss, and as they begin rolling Carson's pretty sure he remembers the truck lighting up eyes of two maybe three animals crouchin' in the brush as they pass.

Next thing he does recall clearly is waking up mid-afternoon in the motel across the highway from my bar and phoning the Sheriff's office. Yes, they'd had his car towed after the County road crew finally spotted it—pretty much buried under snow. A trucker reported his whereabouts; said he'd found a guy wandering in the dark along the South Boundary Road, mumbling about a lost car or something. Later that afternoon a patrolman picks him up, takes his report, and after paying the impoundment fee in Ontonagon, he drives back to Union City. "A couple hours later I walk into your bar," Carson says to me.

Fascinating story, right my friend? Except, that's not the end of it, so let me buy you another round and tell you the rest of the story, as Paul Harvey might say.

Well sir, it's about two-thirty in the morning when Carson finishes up—lookin' totally wiped out across the table—and rests his forehead on the folds of his arms. Then somethin' curious happens: Mountain Man rises real slow, sends a shallow nod my way, and walks around to where Carson's sittin'. He lays one of those gnarled hands on the journalist's back for just a couple seconds, and then without sayin' a word, gets his coat and hat from the pegs by the door and is gone. What was that all about? I'm askin' myself. Carson never looks up all the while. Turns out he'd crashed, so I leave him be 'til I clean up.

As Carson's heading out the door to his motel across the road, he says he'll be gone a few days to shoot pictures of the ice caves and then maybe try to find the Halliwell and capture some images of the two hermits and Hugo. I tell 'im that before he sets out for the mountains there's somethin' real important he's gotta know, but it's late. I put my hand on his shoulder and repeat: "Carson, it's real important; be sure we talk tomorrow before you go lookin' for the Halliwell."

So what's so important? Well, remember I said a flash bulb went off when the journalist started talkin' about two hermits named Gus and George and nephew Hugo? Well, it hit me that his hermits were the Boyer Boys, as locals used to refer to 'em. I say "used to" because the hermits died fifty years ago. And the Halliwell? The State leveled what would've been their shack long about 1964. Too unsafe they figured, if hikers in the Park walked into the abandoned mine site. Gus died first and then George after seven more years up there by himself. How do I know all this for sure? Well... this photo I keep next to my cash register—see the inscription: Hell Well, 1958. The pretty blond teenage gal in the foreground, pretendin' to swill a bottle of beer, well later on she became my first wife; picture's about all I've left of her. She was related to the Boyers through the Stueber clan over by Ironwood. Anyway, see these two geezers on either side of the family at the picnic table? One's smokin' a corn cob pipe; bushy beard's probably coverin' a crooked jaw. The other's got horn rim glasses and a shirt that could be fresh ironed.

So do the math; that picnic happened some fifty-six or so years ago, not too long before those Boys died at the ripe ages of seventy-four and eighty-one. How in hell could Carson have stepped foot into the Halliwell shack or talked with the hermits last winter?

There's one more tidbit: the Mountain Man. I kept watching his reaction as the journalist's spinning out his encounter with the uncles and their nephew.   Then it hit me who he is: Hugo Boyer, the nephew.   Guess you might say he's the last of the Boyer Boys. He's in this photograph, too—tall guy in uniform, maybe in his twenties—behind Gus. Something struck me as familiar when that big guy walked into my bar, but it's been decades.   As I recall, he became quite the ace in the Air Force and flew cargo planes for a while after he resigned his commission. Word around town was that he left the service on good terms, but Hugo always pushed the limits of good old military rules and regs, and he finally got fed up.

He moved back up here after the uncles died. Caused a bit of a ruckus when the State took title to the Halliwell property after George passed. For a while Hugo lived out of the shack, 'til they leveled it, and warned off curious hikers and out-and-out poachers—thieves you might say—who wandered onto the Hell Well.   The still was the first to go, years before, but after George died they stole pretty much all the rifles, steamer trunks of clothes and keepsakes, kitchen stuff, stoves—even the rickety iron beds and soiled mattresses.   I heard tell shots were fired on one occasion, and Hugo was lucky that the old ranger who showed up used to enjoy Gus' fifty cent beef.

For a while after that, I'd sometimes hear stories at bars or deer camp about this hermit, a huge rough-looking guy livin' just beyond State land, deep in the Porkies.   A few of the old timers who still knew their way through the brush might see him stalking the mountain ridges during deer season. Or floatin' in an inflated raft pullin' trout from holes in a stream so thick with alders and old beaver dams that nobody thought could be got to let alone fished. Another story had it that he flushed grouse with a couple big dogs, but at least one guy insisted he'd seen 'im once with coyotes—and a three-legged one at that. More than one claimed to hear of a grizzled mountain man walking up on backpackers' campsites near to daylight, callin'out, "There's bear roamin' nearby," and then remindin' the scrambling Trolls to be sure to hike their food down from the tree before movin' on real fast.

And here's the last thing: I never did get to tell Carson any of that, 'cause I never seen hide nor hair of the journalist again. Owners of the motel told me he checked out a couple days after he and I said goodnight. Can't say if he ever wrote up his story, but I keep my eye out for it or his photos. Some other fella published a glossy book with grand shots of the caves, so I don't know.

The Mountain Man? Haven't seen him either.

Well there it is, my friend—the rest of the story.

Told it before? Breaking news: Bartenders with stories sell more liquor, and around these parts, sadly or not, that's the solid part of our economy these days. So what'll you have? I'm out of Sheep Dip.

23.
How Beautiful It Is
Carmanie Bhatti

1

How beautiful it is spending
time with you Lord, for nothing is
greater than your love, 'tis all I
need, you give me before I ask

2

I wish I could express your love
for me, for you my Parent, knows
my hunger, thirst, passion, needs, wound,
burden, delight, you know it all

3

Let me pause from all that the world
thinks vital, thank my dear Lord who
reminds me I'm not an orphan
and, brings surprises, big or small

4

You're my wonderful friend and hope
I trust and am led toward you
saying, "You know me inside, out,
take care of your child, weak and small"

24.
How Far Can I?
Carmanie Bhatti

1

How far can I extend my hand
to write about my Lord, for I
lack words and expression, I feel
your presence in blessings, when days
are busy and, burdened with fears

2

Can I reach the ends of the world
to tell All, who you are, for I
know you will take my words to dry
and heavy hearts, to give them life

3

I listen to your voice Lord, speak,
for I know you are speaking, I
will write it down, so that people
read about you, your love for them

4

Lord, give me the words, melody,
to sing your composition of
music, so that the tired souls can
sing and dance, as choir, to praise you

25.
I Have Learned To Fear
Carmanie Bhatti

I have learned to fear
the God of Israel whose
love made me alive

The Lord who helped me,
taught me think, that better for us
is to trust in God

It is good to take
refuge in the living God
than to trust in flesh

Now that I do draw
water of life, I have the
Lord God , salvation

I am proclaiming
the name of the blessed Lord with
words of sheer wisdom

May the Triune God
be with me when people hate,
betray, desert me

May the labor of
my hands be a blessing, and
let me slumber not

I am glad to see
God's creation, blessings that
give life, not destroy

My days will be like
that of an evergreen tree
bearing fruit on time

May God be my words,
the words of wisdom, love, peace
and faith to others

26.
I Am From
Ceiligh Cacho-Negrete

I am from the musical instruments,
that my father plays in the early morning and late in the evening,
from the chess board on which I have played out victories and lost,
spectacularly.
I am from the book shelves I have combed,
looking for something new to read.

I am from the tree in my backyard which I played under for years
until my parents cut it down.
I am from the swing set
upon which I have sustained many minor injuries.

I am from the Easter eggs from many Easters ago,
that we can still find in my backyard.
I am from the time I slid down the hill
and hit a tree with my cousins.
I am from pumpkin pie and macaroni and cheese.

I am from Nana and Grandpa,
Granny, Aunt Lottie, my parents
and all those times I've been a bratty older sister
and every time I told my sister I love her.

I am from "Our little secret" and "Put the book down," "Go outside," "Put
the book down," "Play with your sister," "Put the book down," "Talk to
your grandparents,"
"Put the book down," "Put the book down,"
"Put the book down."

I am from the house in North Conway where a little of my spirit still lives,
from the Amesbury Public Library to the Portland Public Library,
and from everywhere in between.
I am from the rusty bridges that I both hate and love
because it means going somewhere else
and means coming home again.

I am from the scrapbook in the farthest corner of my closet
in which I hide my best memories and favorite feelings
so that when I need them they're right there
waiting for me to get lost in them.

27.
Inspired by an Elegy
Michael D. Jones

I strike a match against my shoe.
It is something I saw in a movie
Or read in a book, or heard in a song
You scrape a wooden match stick
(Paper is too flimsy, it must be wood)
So quick, the friction you generate
Forcing the tip across a rough surface
The scuffed bottom of your shoe or heel
The rubbing heat excites the sulphur
Which first begins to glow, then flashes
And, *Whoosh...* the tip sparks into flame
And settles into a slow, even burn
(When you hold the stick just right)
Which is all I need to light this life
Like a prayer candle or big cigar
To push-back against the nothingness
With ambient glow, or halo of light
Or expanding puff of near-white smoke.
Anyhow, it wasn't my idea... *fire.*
Still, in my funeral suit and best shoes
I always travel with a box of matches.

28.
La Guitarra
Terry Sanville

1

My first owner, Gary, brought me home from a music store in Long Beach. The Japanese had just bombed Pearl Harbor. Compared to war, nobody thought playing an instrument was that important. He bought me cheap.

Gary worked as a winch operator at the Port of San Pedro. At night, he'd return exhausted to that tiny house, to his pregnant wife, and to me. He'd slump into his easy chair and down half a quart of Pabst that Marge set out for him. Then she'd take me off the wall and hand me over. He'd twist my push pegs to tune me, pull dog-eared sheet music from under his chair and finger the notes to *Red River Valley* and *Streets of Laredo*. I got so damned tired of those songs I almost snapped my gut strings in protest. My Maker, José, built me for flamenco, not for cowboy chords and bad yodeling. As José pieced me together, he'd told stories about the Spanish masters and I dreamed of being cradled in the arms of Rámon Montoya, or maybe Juan Moreno, filling a Madrid café with my rapid-fire falsetas as the beautiful bailaoras clacked their heels and danced.

But Gary treated me with respect. Every night after practice he'd wipe down my blonde cypress back and sides, buff my French Polished face with a soft piece of flannel, then carefully place me on the wall hook. From there I gazed onto the harbor and watched the freighters come and go, mostly gray Liberty ships loaded with war machines and military supplies. I wondered when he'd get his Greetings letter from the draft board, feared the day when they'd take him away from me.

As Gary's playing improved, my attitude toward Laredo and Texas also improved and our nightly concerts became the day's highpoint. One evening after practice, he sat with Marge on the tattered sofa and talked.

"I'm gonna join the Merchant Marine," he said.

"Why? They need you at the port... and your bosses can get you a draft deferment."

"I don't want them to. Everybody's going and I wanna do my part."

"What am I supposed to do... now that the baby's coming?"

"Your Mother and Sheila can stay with you. They'll wanna get the hell out of Stockton anyway, and your Mom's got plenty of experience with babies. You'll have fun."

"Fun? Really? How'd you like it if I made you live with your Mother?"

Gary grinned. "Yeah, she's a real pistol." He hugged Marge.

She began to cry. "What... what about me? Why do you wanna leave me?"

"Believe me, I don't... but I feel I've got to go."

He took me down from my hook and played chords softly. They continued to talk and cuddle.

For six months Gary trained to be a merchant seaman, in Avalon, on Santa Catalina Island just off the coast from San Pedro. Marge pored over his letters and read them to her mother and sister, leaving out the bedroom parts. She sat outside on the tiny patio that overlooked the harbor and stared offshore. Meanwhile, I gathered cobwebs and became home to a colony of dust mites while hanging on the wall, forgotten. The house held little music – none of the women sang, and their old Motorola radio crackled and hummed and made hardly any sound. All their money seemed to go toward food and rent.

Gary came home from Avalon. After a good cleaning, he played me one last time before he departed on a Liberty ship bound for the Philippines. I felt like weeping and tried to make my music come out clear and sweet. After he left, the days dragged by. The mother and sister had gone to work for Douglas Aircraft, building bombers. I collected more dust. Marge grew large. One night, the moon shifted from behind the clouds and cast her pale light on my wall. Marge let out a scream that rattled my strings. A neighbor owned an old Model T and had enough gas to drive the three women away. After four days, two women and a baby girl returned.

The new grandmother and aunt huddled together on the sofa and sobbed. I wanted to console them, but knew no one who could stroke me to make soothing sounds. They hired a neighbor lady, Rosalina, as a wet nurse and housekeeper and went back to work. When the baby fussed and couldn't be quieted, she'd pluck my strings and sing Mexican songs. She had a wonderful voice, but was no guitarist. She broke my high E-string tuning it too tightly and never played me again. But she'd sing during the hot days with all the windows thrown open and the sea wind breathing new life into our somnolent home.

Gary returned from the Philippines. The Japanese had attacked and sank his ship, leaving most of her crew stranded on Luzon during the invasion. It had taken him weeks to recover and find a berth on a freighter bound for the West Coast. When he arrived in San Pedro, he stayed drunk for the first few days, too late for Marge's funeral, but soon enough to mourn her death. It wasn't long before Gary and the women began fighting. They reminded him that he had thirty days to find another ship assignment or be subject to the draft. They wanted him to pay more money to help raise the child. They had wrapped their lives around providing for the tiny girl and saw no need for an itinerant father. They wanted him gone.

The night before we left, the women and Gary argued loudly. The ruckus sent the baby into a high-pitched squealing fit, in the key of B-flat. The next morning, Gary packed his duffel bag. He replaced my snapped string. At the base of my body he drilled a small hole and inserted a wooden peg. He fastened a strap made from an old leather belt to the peg and tied its other end to my headstock with a shoelace. Slinging me over his shoulder, he picked up his bag and we headed out. I felt free, wanted him to play me as we plodded northward along the coast road, with Gary humming *Red River Valley* all the while.

2

We traveled slowly those first days, Gary walking with his back to traffic, his left thumb extended. He'd grumble and curse, then sob quietly. I tried to focus my thoughts – play me, Gary, play me. But he must have been thinking about Marge and the suffocating loneliness that seemed his fate. He ducked his head against the north wind, leaned forward and trudged up the coast.

We got a few rides, mostly from men involved somehow in the war or from local merchants. They spied his ragged pea coat and took him for a Navy sailor. When a fat old guy found out that Gary served in the Merchant Marine he frowned.

"Ya know, Walter Winchell thinks you guys are a bunch of slackers and draft dodgers. He says you refused to unload ships at Guadal canal... says your bosses are all Commies."

Propped up in the back, I watched Gary's ears turn red. He twisted sideways in his seat and glared at the driver.

"You've got it wrong, buster. We got bombed, strafed, and torpedoed by the Japs... lost a lot of good men hauling supplies to our troops. You... you should be ashamed."

"Hey, I'm just sayin' what I heard."

We got out of that car at the next intersection on the Coast Highway, somewhere south of Ventura. I could feel Gary tremble all over. But that idiot had snapped him out of his stupor. For a while, anger replaced sadness. Camping on the beach that night along the Rincon Coast, he soaked his blistered feet in the cold Pacific, built a driftwood fire, and strummed me hard, like a flamenco master using the Rajeo technique. The silver surf glowed in the moonlight. He wrapped me in an old pillowcase to protect my body from the damp fog that rolled onshore. It helped, but not much. My wood swelled with moisture, only to shrink again when daylight struck me. My internal braces loosened, my face grew tight, and I became afraid.

After hitchhiking most of the next morning, we got a ride from a produce hauler. We spent what felt like forever bouncing along in the back of his truck, stuffed between boxes of cauliflower and peas, and rolled into Santa Barbara late that afternoon. The driver dropped us off near a white beach lined with Palm Trees. A freight train rumbled north on an inland line that bordered the boulevard.

The driver leaned out his window. "Now look, you'd better stay off the streets and the beach at night. The cops or shore patrol will nab ya."

"Got any ideas where I can sleep?" Gary asked.

"There's a hobo jungle in them trees." The driver pointed toward the railroad. "The lady that owns the land lets tramps camp there, but she comes around to make sure everything's kept clean, and she don't allow no drinkin'."

"Thanks for the tip... and the ride."

With a grinding of gears and billowing blue smoke from its tailpipe, the truck pulled away. Gary faced the beach, buffeted by an onshore wind. He shivered then turned and walked inland through the trees. We came to a clearing. A dozen low shanties, built of scrap wood, doors, and window frames, surrounded a garden and a blazing fire pit. Weathered men with hollow cheeks sat in rickety chairs outside each shack. They eyed us suspiciously as we approached. A skinny man forced himself up and hobbled toward us.

"What you want, mister?" he called.

"I'm just looking for a place to sleep. I don't mean to bother anyone."

"You got any booze?"

"No sir."

"That's too damn bad," the old guy said and the hobos laughed. "My name's Joe."

"I'm Gary."

"You some kinda deserter or somethin'?"

"Not me. I'm in the Merchant Marine."

"What the hell you doin' here? They're not shippin nothin' outta Santa Barbara."

"It's a long story."

"You're not some damn spy for the cops, are ya?"

"No, I've got no use for them."

"That's good ta hear. You play that git-tar ya got there?"

"I'm just learning. I know *Red River Valley* and *Streets of Laredo* real well."

Joe flashed a gap-toothed grin. "Good enough. We'll teach ya some new tunes."

"Thanks."

"You can sleep in that shack next to mine. Ole Larry up and died last week so you're in luck. They call me the mayor of this place. Do as I tell ya and you won't get in no trouble."

"I'm not looking for trouble, Joe."

We stayed in the camp for two days, Gary eating beggars stew with the rest of the men and scrounging for food and firewood during the day. At night around the fire, I got passed between rough hands. Crooked fingers formed simple chords that accompanied their high squeaky voices... mountain music they called it. One of the men cradled an ancient banjo in his lap and strummed along. My humble stringed sister seemed happy enough with her lot but kept trying to show me up with fast and loud playing. Gary struggled to keep the beat while the grinning crowd clapped their hands. But in the end, my sweet tone won them over and sets of envious eyes followed Gary's every move. I was glad when we left that place.

Near dawn on the third day we waited next to the railroad, just north of Santa Barbara's depot and the huge fig tree. Joe had given Gary tips on how to jump a moving train. So there was little drama when he heaved his duffel bag into an empty boxcar of a northbound freight and dove headfirst into the opening, with me strapped to his back. He crawled to the front of the car to keep out of the wind. We had the place to ourselves. As the sun came up and the air warmed, the countryside became a blur of golden hills backing up a white-cliff coastline. The sky had cleared and the offshore islands stood out sharply across a glassy sea.

Gary spent the morning writing in his journal, a present from Marge before he'd left for seaman school. The more he scribbled, the more the sadness overtook him. We rolled northward all day, only slowed when passing through San Luis Obispo, then up the Cuesta Grade and onward toward Salinas. At sunset we pulled into a freight yard near a series of wharfs crowded with gray Liberty ships. A huge orange bridge crossed the mouth of the bay, its cables glowing like harp strings in the waning light. We ditched our boxcar and hurried from the yard. In a shabby warehouse district Gary found a tavern and ducked inside. Mariners and longshoremen filled the place. I felt his muscles relax as he moved among his own kind to a corner table. He slumped into a chair and ordered a beer, then another.

While living with Marge, Gary didn't get drunk at home. But that night he looked determined to push the conscious world, including me, far away from him. Two sailors and a civilian sat at our table.

"You mind if we play cards while we wait?" the skinny sailor asked.

"Suit yourself," Gary said.

"You a mariner?" the round sailor asked.

"Yeah, I've just come up from San Pedro."

"You got a ship assignment?" skinny sailor asked.

"Nah, not yet."

"You should try to get on with us. We're on the Daly. She's got a good skipper and crew... not a spit-and-polish bunch."

Gary yawned. "Yeah, I need to check in soon."

"We'll take ya to the office after we're done here," round sailor offered.

"Thanks."

The bartender delivered a bottle and four glasses. The civilian held out his hand to Gary. "My name's Eddie Fulton. I own this bar. Have a drink on me."

"Thanks, Eddie. Ah... nice place."

"Who're you kiddin'? This place is a dump... but it's my dump and you boys keep me in business."

"Happy to oblige," skinny sailor cracked.

Eddie poured a round of drinks and they started playing stud poker, using matches to bet with. As the night wore on, the room filled with smoke and got hot and stuffy. My strings slackened. The card players emptied the first bottle and had nearly finished a second when Gary ran out of money, right when it looked like he could win big. He held a full house, aces over eights, but didn't have enough to call. The other mariners had folded. I knew about poker from the San Pedro women; they used to play for pennies while Gary was away sailing the Pacific.

"Look guys, I'm broke," Gary complained. "Can somebody lend me enough to finish this hand? I'll pay ya back, promise."

The other men stayed quiet. Finally, Eddie cleared his throat. "Throw in that guitar of yours and I'll call it good."

Gary pushed his chair back and stared at Eddie. "I... I can't do that. We've been through a lot. She... she helps me through the day."

"Suit yourself," Eddie said. "So I take it you fold?"

"What... what if you promise to keep the guitar here until I get back from my next assignment. If I lose this hand, I'll buy it back from you then."

"Sure, son." Eddie grinned. "That's fine with me."

Eddie had two queens showing. When he turned over his down cards, four ladies stared up from the table. The color drained from Gary's face. He grasped me for the last time and fingered the notes to our familiar songs before handing me over.

"Sorry, son. But you can buy it from me anytime."

"Don't you worry. Keep her safe and put new strings on her every once in a while. I'll be back."

Eddie hung me from a hook on the wall in back of the bar. From there I could see the entire room and everyone coming and going. The two sailors helped Gary to his feet. He stared at me with teary eyes, a big goofy smile splitting his face. They half lifted him across the room to the heavy front door and pushed outside into a foggy night. Keep warm, friend, and come back to me humming *Red River Valley*.

3

My life as a bar guitar swung from boring to frantic. When the merchant fleet was in, the mariners and longshoremen packed Eddie's Place and the booze flowed like water until closing time. Other nights, Eddie and Donald, the bartender, played a lone game of blackjack in a quiet corner. Neither of them ever took me off my wall hook to play. My strings deadened. I felt my neck warp from the steam heat. Every few days, Donald passed me to some drunken sailor who wanted to impress his buddies or a local whore, and I'd suffer his coarse handling. My face became scratched and dinged and a long crack formed just west of my soundhole. My interior braces continued to loosen; they'd rattle when somebody struck my strings hard.

On a hot August day, the bar filled with yelling and screaming mariners and women, more broads than I'd ever seen in that dive. *The San Francisco Chronicle* headlines shouted "Peace! Japan Surrenders Unconditionally." The sailors kissed their girlfriends and did more, right there in the bar. The next day, word filtered in about the riots on Market Street: windows smashed, businesses looted, and scores of people hurt. But nobody seemed to care – the war was over!

Not a day went by that I didn't watch every patron coming through the tavern's door, hoping that Gary's pink boyish face would appear, that he'd rescue me from that underbelly of city nightlife. In the dark barroom after Eddie had locked up and left to join his wife and baby son, I'd think about San Pedro and Gary's hands cleaning me after every practice session. But those memories felt too painful and I shifted my thoughts to being discovered by some famous flamenco player and whisked away.

The years flowed past, along with another war in some place called Korea. The bar patrons became a texture of faces. I stopped noticing their particular natures and struggled to hold onto a mental image of Gary. Eddie installed a jukebox against the far wall, a chrome and glass Wurlitzer, and the quiet hours that I'd learned to appreciate disappeared. A while later, he moved me aside from my spot, built a sturdy shelf and installed a television for the bar patrons to stare at. In the afternoons, they'd sit on their stools and gaze vacantly into the flickering blue light, muttering under their breaths to the imaginary characters on its screen. I got played less and less and knew my days as a bar guitar were numbered.

During all the years, Eddie changed my strings only once, had fastened the top three to their tuning pegs backwards. He replaced my old gut strings with nylon ones, the bottom three wrapped with silver wire. I sounded wonderful, but hardly anybody played me and I collected dust. Finally, my strings went slack from age. Eddie cut them off, wedged a clock in my sound hole and plugged it into a wall socket. The clock hummed in C-sharp, never changing. I thought I'd go crazy with the noise and die from the shame of becoming a mere wall fixture.

The music from the Jukebox changed. The sound of big band jazz and torch songs gave way to fast-tempo tunes with loud drums and strange-sounding guitars – and ballads like *Love Me Tender* sung by a guy with a vibrato you could throw a cat through.

One morning before opening, Eddie took me down from my wall hook, removed the clock and we left the bar, the first time I'd been outside since the War. He placed me in the back of his car, a long swooping machine with pointed tail fins, and drove to a tiny shop on a side street. A man dressed in a leather apron came to the counter.

Eddie cleared his throat. "I know your sign says violins, but do you repair guitars?"

"That depends. Let me see what you have." The man grasped me gently by the body and gave me a shake that dislodged dust balls from my dirty insides and made my braces rattle. He sighted down my neck and fingered my cracked face.

"I've had this thing since '44," Eddie said. "My wife insists that our boy learn to play an instrument. So I need it repaired.

The man frowned. "It sure has led a rough life. It could cost a pretty penny to fully restore it."

"Yeah, well, what would you recommend?"

"I'd glue the cracked top and braces, add new strings, and clean it up a bit. It should be fine for a beginner."

"All right, let's do that. How much?"

"Thirty dollars plus the cost of strings."

"Jesus, I could order a brand new one from Sears and Roebuck for less than that."

"Maybe, but those things don't sound as good as this one will... if it's fixed properly."

"Is it worth anything?"

"Sorry, I don't know enough about guitar builders to tell you."

"Okay, go ahead."

"It'll be finished next Thursday."

I felt nervous. Would this guy repair me or destroy me, give me back to Eddie a crippled wreck never to be played again? The man took me to the rear of his shop and laid me on a workbench. I prepared myself for the gluing and restringing process, but not for what happened over the following week. He removed all of my fret wires and heated my warped neck with a blistering hot iron, then clamped a vice-like machine to my neck that straightened it. He sanded my fingerboard until it was perfectly level, installed new nickel silver frets, glued my face cracks, cleaned my body, and rubbed new shellac all over me until I shone like clear glass.

When Eddie came to pick me up his mouth dropped open. "What the hell did you do?"

"I decided to do more work than what we talked about. I need the practice. I have a feeling guitar repair is going to become a lucrative business."

"So how much is all this gonna cost me?"

"Thirty dollars plus two bucks for the strings."

Eddie grinned, his once-smooth face now spider-webbed with wrinkles, and reached for his wallet.

"You should buy a case for it. I don't have any here, but there's a place on Van Ness that sells them, very reasonable."

"Thanks, I'll do that."

Back in the car, I felt like I'd just come off my Maker's workbench. My whole body rumbled in sync with the vibrations of Eddie's Chevy. We drove across San Francisco to a neighborhood with two-story houses set back from the street and overlooking a huge swath of trees and grass. Eddie's boy, Pete, met us at the door, grabbed me and ran upstairs to his corner bedroom. A window looked out onto what I would learn to be Golden Gate Park and the bay beyond.

I hadn't been around children much so I didn't know what to expect. Unlike his father, Pete stood maybe five feet tall in his tennis shoes, with a skinny waist, slender arms, and small hands and fingers. He'd have difficulty playing barre chords on me. Pete shut the door to his room, sat on the bed and fingered my strings, his touch clumsy but light. By the time his mother called him to dinner, he'd figured out how to tune me and to finger a G and E-minor chord, all without help from sheet music or books. I had a good feeling about him when he took a clean T-shirt from a drawer and wiped me down. It reminded me of Gary so long ago. I could feel Pete's excitement of discovering music as a performer. I felt wanted again and reveled in the sounds I made, as if hearing myself for the first time.

4

In the years that followed, Eddie bought his son guitar instruction books by Mel Bay and others. One of the books included *Red River Valley*. Pete learned it quickly and sang the verses in a sweet tenor voice. Hearing that song, I almost felt that my life would repeat itself and half expected the boy to leave home on a hitchhiking adventure along the coast.

Pete practiced every day for at least two hours and often longer. He learned to read notes and chord symbols, and liked music books filled with folk tunes where he could fingerpick and strum me while he sang. But as he got older, his musical tastes changed and he tuned in rock-and-roll stations on his radio, bought record albums, and used me to play along with that raucous noise. He learned barre chords and figured out how to finger arpeggios. But I wasn't built to make that kind of sound. I knew something would change, and not in my favor.

Pete grew his hair long, something his father detested but his mother tolerated. After pleading with them for months, his parents bought him a cherry-red Gibson electric guitar and a tweed-covered amplifier. The Gibson had a broad face, f-holes like a violin, lots of chrome knobs and switches, and a long skinny neck with pearl inlays. He'd play her for hours, practicing fast arpeggios, but still playing finger style. A neighborhood boy with a bass guitar joined him and they'd play and sing until Pete's mom banged on the door and screamed at them to keep it down.

Pete propped me in a corner of his room. I felt unloved, and despaired that I'd never compete with the Gibson and the blasting sounds coming from the amps. But his mother kept me dusted and cleaned and away from direct sunlight. The room felt cool, but not cold, so my neck and body didn't shrink or swell like it had in Eddie's Place. One day, Pete and his mom packed suitcases full of his clothes and boyhood treasures. Eddie brought home a guitar case and slipped me inside its plush burgundy interior. From arguments between Pete and his parents, I'd learned that he'd be living in a dormitory on the UC Berkeley campus across the bay, and that the school didn't allow electric guitars in the dorm rooms. So I would be accompanying my owner to college.

Pete studied architecture. But every chance he got, he walked Telegraph Avenue and played me in storefronts for spare change. The country was involved in yet another conflict, this one in a far-off corner of Southeast Asia. He became one of the many protesting Vietnam. Unlike my first owner, Pete had no interest in doing his part to support the war. His part became that of a protester, and I helped voice his discontent. He carried me everywhere and sang raw-edged songs that berated the 'masters of war.'

On a blustery day in May, we moved toward People's Park to join a throng of students railing against the University for ripping out landscaping and preparing to construct buildings on the land. I thought it strange that Pete would protest since he studied architecture, the art of building stuff. But I'd learned that humans are anything but consistent.

The crowd continued to swell. Pete slipped my strap over his shoulder and sang a Dylan song. A horde of Police advanced on the students, firing gas canisters into the crowd that made the kids choke and vomit like drunks on a three-day binge. The officers wore helmets and masks and carried shields. They pushed into the throng, swinging their clubs and chasing the protesters down Telegraph Avenue. Pete slung me across his back, turned and ran toward the junior high school several blocks away. People streamed past us, screaming, holding their bloodied heads. The police raised guns to their shoulders and fired. A boy running next to us dropped, the right side of his shirt shredded. Pete picked up speed and dodged and weaved. Others near us were hit and staggered into the neighborhood. An officer ran after us with his gun held before him, his shoes slapping against the pavement. He pulled up short and raised his weapon. Pete glanced over his shoulder then turned to face the officer, protecting me with his body. The man fired. The blast caught Pete in the left arm, from his shoulder to his wrist. Bits of hot metal pierced his flesh and broke through my back. I felt his warm blood flow into my body, staining my wood.

The blast spun Pete around. He took off down a side street, gripping his arm and groaning. Pete found a pay phone and called his parents, who whisked us to a nearby hospital then across the bay to their home. I rested in my old corner of his bedroom while he recovered. The doctors encouraged him to play me as a way of strengthening his muscles and tendons. At first, fingering the simplest chords caused him great pain. But as the weeks passed his dexterity and confidence returned.

One day, his father watched him practice. "That old guitar looks like hell. You want me to get it fixed?"

Pete rubbed his fingers across the holes in my back, the wood splintered and stained by his blood. "Hell no. I want people to know what those pigs did to us. They can't kill my axe or me. She's too strong for them."

"Yeah, well they came too damn close. You have to stop hanging around with those hippie rabble-rousers. You'll get yourself killed."

"The Army will get me killed if I drop out of school and get drafted."

"You're right about that. But you're probably 4-F anyway, with that arm. I wouldn't worry about going to war anytime soon."

"Maybe not. But there's always the next one, right Pop?"

Eddie ran a hand through his gray hair and nodded.

5

In the autumn of 1969, Pete returned to college and took me and the Gibson with him. We avoided protest rallies. He ignored me, spending all his time hunched over a drafting board in his backstreet apartment with psychedelic rock blasting from huge speakers.

In two years, he graduated with honors. He landed a job with a large Oakland firm, met a wonderful woman named Joyce and got married. We lived in the hills overlooking the San Francisco Bay. The Gibson and I occupied our own spots in a wall-to-wall carpeted living room that opened onto a protected patio. Pete played me every night after work, just like Gary had done in San Pedro so many years before. But instead of guzzling cheap beer and playing *Red River Valley*, he drank scotch, studied classical arrangements by Andrés Segovia, and struggled to master Brazilian jazz with all its damned finger-cramping chords.

I never felt ignored or unloved. But that didn't stop me from becoming shamefully jealous of my sister guitar, the Gibson. While Pete used me to study music, he played the electric for the power and energy that she gave him. I wanted to feel that energy, that emotional sting from the music, but knew I couldn't compete. My envy increased when they began playing electric blues, songs with lots of string bending and vibrato. Somehow those sounds struck at my flamenco soul and I wept inside while the Gibson seemed to revel in her raw magic.

Joyce gave Pete two children, a hulking son named Erick and a shy daughter named Lily. As they grew, I expected them to mess around with the Gibson and myself. But they and their friends seemed content with being listeners rather than performers. They liked the chicka-chicka songs of some British band with a funny name that sounded like The Heebie Jeebies. Then there was a tune where screaming voices melded perfectly into a screaming guitar solo—sounding like the high shriek from a freight train's brakes. I knew the Gibson loved that crap, which made me despise her, but not for long. I suppose my own mellow music rankled her down-and-dirty sensibilities.

The children left for college, somewhere back east. One night, with the fog smothering the bay with gray cotton candy, Erick returned. He wore a camouflaged soldier's uniform. Joyce cried when she saw her son, but left the two men alone to talk.

"Didn't I teach you anything?" Pete demanded. "The '60s wasn't just some damn aberration, ya know... and you could have become anything you wanted. But a soldier?"

"It's different now, Pop. We have to do something or that fucking Saddam will do more than just invade Kuwait."

"You know, it's all bullshit, all about oil, don't you?"

"No, it's about doing the right thing. If we need to be the cops of the world, then so be it. Better us than the Russians."

They argued over multiple scotches and beers. Finally, Erick left the house to join his Army buddies at a local tavern. Pete went to a hall closet and dug out all of his old songbooks. We played Dylan, Donovan, and Buffy Saint-Marie songs until Joyce came in and helped her drunken husband to bed. My strings vibrated all that night with the sudden infusion of energy, and with the sorrow of knowing that history would indeed repeat itself.

Desert Storm ended quickly, Erick survived unscathed, and the books full of protest songs were again squirreled away, only to be retrieved on nights when Joyce attended Art Guild meetings and Pete had the house to himself. His fine tenor voice stayed strong throughout middle age and into his graying years.

After three decades of work, he and Joyce moved south to San Luis Obispo. He took a teaching post at Cal Poly University. Myself and the Gibson had our own air-conditioned music room with a huge window looking out onto the broad Edna Valley. Pete and Joyce became involved with the University's La Guitarra Celebration. This past year he drove to the airport to pick up a flamenco guitarist who would stay at the house during the festival. Rámon would play that night at the Performing Arts Center. My strings tightened with excitement.

When Pete and Rámon arrived at the house, there was a huge commotion with much wailing and anguished cries from the men and Joyce. They entered the music room. Pete placed a mangled guitar case in the middle of the floor and backed away, shaking his head. Rámon had set the case down in the airport's parking lot to help Pete load the Mercedes's trunk with his luggage. A neighboring car had backed over it. Rámon opened the case and let out a sob. The devastation sickened me and I think the Gibson also felt it because her strings quivered for a moment. The car had crushed the body and splintered the neck, destroying the flamenco instrument.

Rámon slumped into a chair. Pete fixed him a drink. He downed it and asked for another. "I'm supposed to play in two hours. How will I ever find..."

"What about some of the other performers? Could one of them lend you–"

"I doubt it," Rámon snapped. "They won't like the way I tap on the face of their guitar. Besides, they play classical instruments. Most of them sound too muddy to me."

Rámon took a long pull on his drink, leaned back and squeezed his eyes shut. When he opened them, he scanned the room. His gaze came to rest on me, sitting in my stand. His eyes narrowed.

"What is that?" he asked, pointing.

Pete grinned. "That's my old college guitar. We've been through the wars."

"No, it's more than that. Those friction tuning pegs haven't been used for many years."

"You want to look at her?"

"Yes, please."

Pete picked me up, adjusted the tuners and handed me over. Rámon stared into my sound hole. His eyes grew large.

"Do you realize what you have here?"

Pete chuckled. "Yeah, a beat-to-shit guitar with buckshot holes in her back. You can still see my bloodstains inside."

"This... this is a very fine instrument... built by José Ramirez... probably in the 1930s."

"Really? I knew she was old but–"

A rapid-fire arpeggio interrupted Pete's question. Rámon leaned forward, his fingers flying over my fingerboard then tapping my face in the style my Maker had built me for. Every part of my body shivered. Pete left us while Rámon learned all my idiosyncrasies, and I had plenty. He affixed a capo to my neck and played high notes, listening as each rang true to pitch.

I wasn't used to someone beating on my face with his hard fingers. But the drumming awakened images of slender women in bright dresses, arms curved, moving slowly in a circle, heels striking the floor to a fast clapping beat. I could feel my entire body sing.

Rámon neither ate nor drank anything more. Pete drove us to the concert hall and left us in the dressing room. A low rumble from the assembling crowd jangled my nerves. A troop of three women squeezed into the room. Each hugged Rámon.

"We heard what happened," one said. "We're so sorry. That guitar was your pride and joy."

"Yes, yes she was," he answered. "But I have a new friend, at least for tonight." He removed the soft cloth that he'd draped over my body.

The women gasped. "Look at the poor thing," one said. She fingered my face gently then ran a hand with polished nails over the holes in my back.

"She looks wounded," said another.

"Yes, she's no beauty. But she plays and sounds—"

In the background someone spoke in a booming voice. The women checked their makeup in the mirror and hurried out. Rámon tuned me one last time and followed them. We waited off-stage while the announcer finished his introduction. The house lights dimmed and burning white spotlights lit the glistening stage. Rámon moved toward a lone chair, to thunderous applause. He lowered his slight body onto the seat and began playing me immediately. The women followed, two clapping and one dancing.

I struggled to keep my friction pegs in place. I'd be damned if I'd let myself go out of tune. A firestorm of notes echoed throughout the hall. I heard gasps and moans from the audience. As we played, each dancer took her turn: back arched, head held proudly, hands twisting at the wrists, fingers caressing the air slowly, then the quick turns, the gown raised, and the drumming of Spanish leather heels against the hard stage.

Yet in all that emotion and grandeur, with my life's dream fulfilled, I couldn't help but remember the *Red River Valley* and Gary's boyish face grinning with each imperfect note.

29.
Late Winter Ice Storm
Michael D. Jones

Empty roads slide past
February's frozen buds
Rabbits in their den.

30.
Lone Pony
Jon Moray

I gassed up my SUV for a trip to the Old West to fulfill my fantasy of being a cowboy. I drove out onto interstates and motored low on highways, en route to a town forgotten by civilization but discovered by me, thanks to a long, sleepless night and an extensive Google search. That afternoon, I cruised into a one-horse town named Lone Pony, and discovered all of the town folk had suffered from sore throats. I pulled up to a saloon to get a haircut, only to be told I was literally illiterate. I walked down the dusty terrain and found a barber that could make the cut.

"Having a bad hair day?" asked the smart mouth proprietor, as I passed through the vented, double swinging doors. "Yes, my pet rabbit bit me," I matched wits, and pointed to my bandaged index finger." He rolled his eyes at my reply. I noticed he also rolled his R's when he spoke with an accent. The barber cut, clipped, and butchered my hair, so I asked him to cut me some slack.

After the hair cut, I moseyed on to a hotel called the *All The Way Inn*, where I saw a horse outside tied to a wooden hitching rail. The horse was lapping from a trough when I encroached upon it. I gently stroked it's dirt brown mane when I was approached by a man with a glistening silver star on his rawhide vest.

"Son, you don't know what you just stumbled into," said the man, with a pronounced rasp, who introduced himself as the sheriff of Lone Pony. He wore an eye patch, which made me wonder why, but I thought it better to mind my P's and Q's and let it be, thinking he probably suffered the deformity from his ex, you see.

"How's that?" I asked, wiping the excess hair clippings off my neck.

"That there horse belonged to Cowboy Carl, the fastest gun in these parts, that is, before he kicked the bucket last night while entertaining his gal."

"So," I gritted, scowled, and spit to display my toughness, even though I was more of a chicken... until someone ruffles my feathers, and then I really run afoul.

"Carl had a showdown tomorrow at high noon with Flesh Wound Philip, the fastest gun in those parts," he extended a broken pointer toward the western mountains over yonder. "The townspeople and I reckoned the next person that laid hands on Carl's horse would take on Flesh Wound in his place. That person is you, Mr.?"

"Cohol, Ricochet Rick Cohol," I stated, pleased with my impromptu nickname, and squinting my eyes as if I was looking into a solar eclipse. The sheriff could tell from my accent I was a dude from the Old States. I looked at my new stallion and asked the lawman why he is always lapping from the trough.

"That's not water, it's beer. It's your horse now, what are you going to name it?"

I rubbed my chin in thought. "I will name it Al, after my dad, who also had a drinking problem."

"You could lead a horse to drink but you cannot make it stop," the sheriff joked, and bid me goodnight.

Here I was, an unsalted, wanna-be cowboy and my beer chugging horse, to escort me to a showdown. I had never shot a gun before in my life. I shot a deer once on a hunting trip, but never a gun. I scared up the guts to take on this challenge and I wasn't about to pass the buck, even though I had plenty of dough.

Besides the horse, I also inherited Carl's hotel room that he paid up for the week, which was perfect for my feeble self. On my way to the room I was stopped by the same woman he spent his last moments with. "Are you looking for a good time?" she winked, instantly taking a fancy to me. Evidently, I also inherited his gal.

I looked at my wrist watch. "I guess so, there is something wrong with the second hand," I said, swearing I'd never buy used merchandise again. She angrily stomped off, displaying a wide spectrum of colorful language that rendered me red-eyed, blue in the face, and green with envy.

I made my way to the room and checked the closet. Carl left a fine array of cowboy duds that I picked out for tomorrow's showdown; a black denim button down shirt, leather wrangler pants, a deep blue suede vest, and snakeskin boots. On the coat rack was his leather belt and holster with two guns, spurs, and one blood stained white felt cowboy hat with three bullet holes in it.

I lied down looking up at a mirrored ceiling while reflecting on how I would fare against Flesh Wound. The bed sheets were scratchy, like sandpaper, and the mattress was lumpy, like sleeping on a camel, even though I don't smoke cigarettes. I was only able to get forty-five minutes of shut-eye; it's a good thing I sleep with my eyes open.

I got up, rinsed off, and dressed for my date with destiny. I exited the hotel and untied Al, who was, you guessed it, lapping from the trough. He was a grade A horse that needed AA. I hopped on the saddle, kicked the stirrups, and away we went.

I stopped for some grub at a diner and ordered bacon, eggs, and O.J. to wet my beak. Dinah, my server, returned moments later with my beverage that she clumsily spilled on my lap while trying to place it on the table.

"It's looks like drinks are on me," I snickered under my breath. She frowned and fetched my meal.

In a snap, I made quick work of my breakfast and then motioned the waitress over.

"Ready for your check?" she asked, as bland as my meal.

"Check? You mean I get paid to eat here?"

She huffed, made a snide remark, and told me to pay at the register. I went to pay the bill, but he was in the john, so I paid the waitress and thanked her for her sub-par service. Her words cut like a knife and I wondered if a lack of spooning might've been the reason for her bitter demeanor. I shook off the thought and just forked over the loot. I gave her a dollar tip and pocketed the rest of the torn currency, amid a flurry of expletives that would make an outlaw wince.

Galloping on, I passed a final resting place called the Dead Tired Cemetery, where an energetic employee working a shovel, motioned me over and comically explained Flesh Wound ordered him to prepare my grave in advance.

"I can see you really dig your job," I said, in reply. He balled his fists and I can tell he was about to throw them at me, until I flashed my six gun, and told him it was fully loaded. Little did he know when I said "it", I meant Al, my inebriated horse.

I rode on, or should I say, my horse rumbled, bumbled, and stumbled towards the edge of town where the showdown was to take place. Al stopped when tumbleweed crossed its path and proceeded to eat up the rolling plant. It turned out my horse also had a drug problem.

A poster nailed up in front of the wood facade general store piqued my interest. It read "Wanted - Hellish Horace Help - Dead or Alive - Inquire Within." I got a hankering to go inside and apply when a wrangler that sat with his hat covering half of his face, and creaking on a rocking chair proclaimed, "Today is your dying day, Ricochet." His cracking voice creaked in harmony with the chair.

"Don't pay him no mind," the sheriff appeared. "That's Crickety Curt, forever making predictions. He's always in that chair and it never stops creaking."

"I'd say the general store has a major loitering problem. How accurate is he?"

"About 100%," the sheriff admitted, tugging on the burgundy bandanna he wore around his neck. Crickety chuckled as if he had rocks in his mouth. I tugged the reins and Al crept on at a slow gait.

The townspeople lined both sides of the dirt street, offering encouraging, thoughtful words and discouraging, helpless looks. They collectively wiped their faces, nervously awaiting the shootout, and emitting the unwelcoming aroma of day old filth.

As I drew near, I spied Flesh Wound, imposing and statuesque, awaiting my arrival. He wore a long black leather coat and a black beaver-fur hat with a wide brim that complemented the rest of his attire. Legend has it the Grim Reaper employs his services to carry out his dirty work, and Flesh Wound makes quite a killing doing it. His scowl and the unrelenting scorching sun left me soaked in perspiration, dampening my unmentionables. His shadow alone was enough to scare off most, but luck was on my side in the form of my pet rabbit's foot, tied to my belt, that I cut off as an equalizer for the assault on my finger.

Flesh Wound's light eyes burned with fire that I couldn't hold a candle to. "You are target practice. I didn't think you or anyone would show up to this showdown," he laughed, as if he was adding sound effects to a ghost story, while twirling Cimarron's in both hands. If he could shoot a gun as well as he was shooting his mouth, I was in a heap of trouble.

I mustered up the courage to catch up with his showboating and relished the chance to make quick work of this hotdog. I got off my high horse and matched his theatrics with some slick gun juggling of my own. One of the guns went off and a bullet traveled dangerously close to a lady bystander. The near miss was almost a hit. I apologized and returned my focus back toward Flesh Wound.

A sin-buster offered last rites in my direction, that made me second guess my bravery for a minute and perhaps take the first left out of town.

Suddenly, a cowpoke wearing a ten gallon hat, with only an ounce of brains, and less than a pint of patience, announced he would be the one conducting the countdown, and right now. The sheriff barked out final instructions, and summoned the man to start at ten and end at one, as a coyote howled off in the distance.

The man began, "Ten, nine, six, four, fifteen, eight, three, seven, one," and Flesh Wound fired. His bullet hit the barrel of the Colt 45 I was holding in my left hand that set my pistol off firing a shot that ricocheted off the saddle on my horse and then caromed off Flesh Wound's Indian crafted belt buckle. Al sobered up quicker than greased lightning and produced a puddle of piss that almost caused a flood.

An eerie silence filled the air as the gravedigger stopped digging, Crickety stopped creaking, and the coyote stopped howling. The sheriff carefully calculated the sequence of shots. He took into account the shooting experience that divided us, carried the one fact that the man counting wasn't good with numbers, and equally summed up the affair would end in a draw. He also added he was relieved no one got hurt.

"Sakes alive, this is the first time I've been shot. That's a mighty fine piece of gun play, as fine as cream gravy, Ricochet. I don't suppose I could buy you a drink," commented Flesh Wound, with a tip of his hat.

"Much obliged, no thanks, but I think my horse could use one," I said, pointing to Al, shivering like a short-sleeved Floridian on an Alaskan winter cruise.

31.
My Lord Is My Friend
Carmanie Bhatti

My Lord is my friend,
a stronghold for me oppressed,
who forsake me not

I saw the nations
rebuked by God, who made
enemies vanish

My Lord forgot not
my cry, but judged the world with
righteousness, fairness

So, I ask you God
give me the armor, belt, shoes,
shield, breastplate, and sword

Give me the helmet,
teach me to pray in spirit
to give you thanks, praise

Let my dear Lord rise !
Let the nations know that you
are gracious, mighty !

Let me be strong Lord
to open my mouth boldly,
to proclaim you God

32.
Never Too Old For Snow!
Deborah Guzzi

Like a blustering old man the storm
spews snow epitaphs of disregard
for the minions of man. A light froth

falls from the north distant and dry
making muttonchop sideburns on
the bark of barren tree trunks.

The weight of snow bows the trees
downward in tilted dismay. Yet,
the day calls to the young and

through slamming back doors they run
toboggans and saucers in their arms
bundled all round, ah, for my flexible flyer!

33.
Nina
Dennis Klotz

It was one of those cool bleak days that was customary to the coast of Puget Sound in September when the rains worsened. The weekend had been spent cleaning the place, arranging important things in convenient locations; the china, the heirlooms, the photo albums and all of the necessary paperwork had been put in their respective places. She did not want to be a burden. Her eyes were a wash of blue and gray and fluctuated between them in accordance with her mood. Sad soulful eyes, they called them. They looked out to the shore, to the dock where she spent countless vivid hours of her girlhood watching the rising and setting of the sun and listening in blissful solitude to the roaring of the waves at high tide. The water had always looked mysterious and foreboding to her, as if it could just swallow her up, but it was where she felt the most at home and at peace.

Puget Sound was where Nina had spent all of her life, and she felt the sea and the Cascades deep in her bones as if they were a part of her. She felt the pines and the estuaries, felt their rhythms as the seasons transitioned one into another, felt the humming of the ages within them. Sometimes when no one was around, she listened, as if waiting for them to speak to her the secrets of their mystery, waiting for the revelations, the truths lost to time, passed down in legends, wondrous and elusive.

Nina had put on her best dress, the blue one which was her favorite. She thought it fitting that she should look good, on her birthday no less. Nina looked at herself in the mirror above the bureau. She brushed her hair back. The roots were whiter than last time. She ran her hand over her cheek where time had etched the wrinkles into her. She closed her eyes and remembered when she first wore it. It seemed so long ago. Her dress still fit her, though it felt looser on her and she felt less becoming in it. But the dress had not changed, only the woman wearing it. She looked out to the water again. Soon, she thought.

Nina sat down with a pen and her favorite stationary. She had bought it in town years ago and decided she would only use it for special friends on special occasions, but as the years went on she found herself writing on it less and less. She wrote for a long while and then she went outside.

It was cool now on the porch, and she could see the waves getting bigger as they crashed on the shore.   She was the mother of three children; two of them still-born, and a son, now a man of thirty who lived abroad and wrote her on the significant holidays of the year. He had spent a violent restless youth in and out of jail and he called her selfish when she begged him not to leave her; —a widow approaching fifty— for impulsive hedonistic adventures in foreign countries. She used to save the postcards he sent from Paris, London, Tokyo and Moscow, but they became less and less frequent and then they stopped all together. He had always been distant and she had wondered then if she had lost him as she had lost many meaningful things. Nina thumbed her letter in her wrinkled hand. It makes no difference now, she thought.

The wind had picked up and she heard the low boom of thunder in the distance. The screen door opened and snapped shut in the gust and the wind chimes rattled in aggressive dolorous tones. She placed the letter in an envelope and fastened it between the doors before making her way down to the beach. The cool damp earth prickled her bare feet and she was chilled and wet in the rain.

Nina passed the wooden table and the hand-painted chairs and she thought of her neighbors who used to sit with her and read and talk of their happy contended lives. She had tried to conceal it from them as long as she could, but when they did not stop asking her why she slept so much, why she did not work, why she was losing weight, she retreated into her solitude and then they did not call her or ask her questions. When she would run into them at the grocery store and the shops in town, she always heard their voices whispering indiscreetly amongst themselves as she walked away. She knew they talked and they did not try to hide it, but Nina was okay with that. Let them guess. Sometimes it's better if they don't know.

It had hurt her marriage too and she often wondered why he stayed in such a hopeless situation. It was subtle at first, and he would ask her if she was okay. "I'm fine." Nina would say, looking out at the sea. "Just thinking." The sunny days were always the most unbearable, for on those days she felt her lonesome malady accentuated, her silent privation made all the more apparent and felt her own unnaturalness mocked by the natural cheeriness of the summer warmth. Nina felt better in autumn, and it was when she had more time to herself, while her husband fished the waters during the salmon season. He was supportive at first, and the first few years after they had married were the happiest ones she'd known. They were younger then, and that was before it had worn itself into her like a frost. She tried not to cry around him, but sometimes while looking at the sea or the great peaks of Mount Rainier, she could not help herself and the tears would stream uncontrollably. It had been six years since they put him in the ground and she thought of him whenever she laid flowers at his grave on the last Thursday of the month.

She walked out to the dock and the rain came at her from all sides now. The sky was a clouded gray in every direction and her dress blew in the wind as she looked out to where the rough waves devoured the opposite shore. Nina was used to the frigid waters, and she swam them often, even on the coldest of days. She had heard her husband talk of what happens to the fishermen when they fall in during a storm, how they hyperventilate and panic when they hit the water, how their mind goes numb and they lose control of cognitive functions. But it wasn't the coldness that scared Nina.

It wasn't the hypothermia or the shock and the pain of it. What scared her more was the bleakness of the years ahead, the scourge and the numbness of it all. She saw the twilight of her life, saw it flickering on the swollen crests of the waves, saw the blackness in them and felt the autumn rain sharp and cold on her skin. Nina had made up her mind and her resolve to relinquish herself from that pain was never more apparent than when she looked out to those dark waves. She took a deep fleeting breath and dove in.

It was colder than she had anticipated, and the waves were very powerful and violent. She had always been a good swimmer and she swam as hard as she could, but the waves kept pushing her back towards the shore. There was the salty taste of the water in her mouth and it reminded her of tears. She gasped for air and struggled in the water as the waves pounded relentlessly against her. There was lightning and the howling drone of the wind. She could hear it calling her, drawing her out towards the open churning water. Nina, it called. Nina. She pressed out and broke through to the wide open expanse of sea.

The thunder boomed again and Nina could feel herself starting to tire when she looked back to the shore. She was farther out than she had thought, and the cabin was a faint dot in the rain. Above it the snowcapped peaks of Mount Rainier stood proud and majestic in the storm.

I'm sorry for my dreams and all the things I could have been. I'm sorry for my hurt and the way I've hurt. I'm going home now. I'm going home.

The initial sting had been replaced by a cold throbbing sensation and the world seemed to move at a slower and slower pace. She swam until her arms could not carry her and then she slipped silently into the deep as the waves overtook her.

Nina awoke shivering and breathless with a warm blanket around her and she looked up to a face she did not recognize.

"You're lucky to be alive. He waded in the waves for the better part of an hour to bring you back."

"Who did?" she inquired, disoriented and still shaking.

"Your son. He had a gift for you. Something from France," the man said.

"Where is he?" she asked. The shock had come back to her now and Nina felt for the first time that day an ominous terror rising through her. But the man only looked down and shook his head.

"We couldn't resuscitate him."

34.
North Texas Rain
Michael D. Jones

For Cousin Angela

Hard rain for days, thick as bees
Flooding nightly on the national news
All spring; the riverbeds swollen full
Roads washed out, forty plus head
At Red River Breaks gone missing
And now your twin sister, Virginia
After her long battle has gone beyond
Our grasp, beyond plain and hillcrest.
It used to be weddings and birthdays
Now I only ever see you at funerals
So when you call days before her
Memorial service to verify the dates
Of our grandparents deaths, long ago
And you need to get off the phone
As it is raining again, the steady drone
On your roof and windows is calling
You hold me in silence for a breath
And I hear the rain in North Texas.

35.
Not Quite Candyland
Melissa Grunow

Dad stood against the sink in the kitchen, his head lowered and face shadowed by the overhanging lamp. In his hand was a glass with what looked to be swirls of caramel, sweet and aromatic, a liquid that popped as it mixed with the cracked ice. Mom sat in an armchair wearing a fringed leather jacket, pulled photographs away from their sticky album pages, and shoved them in a pocket on the side of her purse. A lone suitcase and an overstuffed duffle bag slumped against the front door. October winds rattled the thin windows and wooshed against the metal siding of our trailer. I shivered in my thermal pull-over, my bare feet cold at the toes, while I sat in a chair on the other side of the living room and picked at the charred edges of a cigarette burn in the seat cushion. From there I watched my parents carefully, breathing their tension and anger, but I remained unnoticed.

I heard my dad pace about the kitchen and the back hallway, and caught glimpses of a hunched figure that never let go of his glass, who sipped it down carefully until all that remained was a subtle pool of watered-down scotch. My two-year-old sister wrapped her dolls in her yellow blankie and put them to sleep in a broken laundry basket next to a tall bookcase lined with Stephen King novels, the Enclopedia Brittanica, and a toppling pile of board games in fraying boxes. My five-year-old brother scooted forward toward the TV, reached up, and turned the knob to a different channel. The screen momentarily turned to snow, then hummed and buzzed to life. He settled in with one of Grandma's crocheted Afghans slung around his shoulders and gnawed through a Tootsie Pop, making me long for some candy of my own.

My gaze turned back to my mother. I knew what was happening, even though I didn't understand it. I tried to conjure up tears, to dig down deep and bring an eruption of emotion to the surface, but I couldn't. Instead, I stared. It was like I was performing, that if I sat a certain way, looked a certain way, caught her eye a certain way, that she would look at me and see me there, see through me there, and tell me she didn't want to leave me behind. I can't remember ever being surprised or shocked by circumstances as a child, and to an eight-year-old me, my mother leaving was just that: it was a circumstance, a situation, a bigger something that was beyond my control.

A car horn sounded in the driveway, and all of us—except my dad—looked to the front door, then the three of us kids looked at my mom. Her face was steady and accepting. She stepped around my sister as she moved to the front door, mechanically reaching down and tucking the edge of the yellow blanket back in through the broken grooves of the basket. My sister grinned up at her, the chocolate frosting from dinner's desert stuck to her cheeks. Mom quietly spoke to a man through the screen, a man whose hand reached in, wrapped around the handle, and pulled the suitcase through the door, his face hidden in darkness.

Days later, still dressed in his fast food restaurant manager's uniform, Dad sat in a lacquered wood chair at the dining table and interviewed a fat woman with a crass voice. His forehead remained relaxed while he held a clenched jaw and wrote notes on her resume. She flipped her hair or widened her eyes under dark, unkempt eyebrows each time she emphasized a point. Her name was Pam, and she was willing to babysit the three of us in our home, not hers, as long as she could bring her toddler. Dad was out of vacation time and out of applicants, so he agreed.

Pam arrived early each morning when my dad was supposed to leave for work, though he would be sleeping through the alarm that buzzed loudly through his closed door. There was still darkness outside the frost-covered windows, and the yellowed lamps illuminated a morning glow.

Throughout the day, Pam sat on the couch crunching on snack foods, the crumbs falling between the cushions. She fed her daughter canned soup from our pantry, leaving my brother and me to prepare lunch for ourselves. I wasn't old enough to use the stove, so I put a can of soup in a shallow pot and stuck it in the microwave. The kitchen had just started to fill with smoke, the edges of the pan not yet sparking, when Pam happened into the kitchen, shouted, and pushed the red button on the front of the microwave.

"You can't put metal in there!"

I blinked back tears and looked at the floor. "I was hungry."

"It will start a fire. You can't use anything metal in a microwave. Not a pan, a fork, or tin foil." She ticked the list of things off on her chubby finger tips, her voice filling the tiny kitchen around us, her furry eyebrows bouncing into her hairline and down again like caterpillars spilling over her forehead.

I nodded.

Pam shifted her weight, moved toward the kitchen sink, and turned on the faucet to fill a plastic cup to the brim. "Have a few sips of water," she said. "That will keep you full until dinner." She handed me the cup and poured the contents of the microwaved pan down the drain. With a flip of the switch to the garbage disposal, I imagined the bits of noodle and chicken swallowed up by the house and washed away.

At night, after work, my dad would play Barry Manilow on his reel-to-reel and sing along with it. Lying in bed, I could sometimes hear the churning of the washing machine or the clattering of dishes being loaded into the dishwasher. He would stay up really late, the reel-to-reel playing the same songs over and over, the washing machine agitating and churning, a faucet running, a closet door closing and his music and his noise would put me to sleep.

In the middle of the night, my dad's silence would wake me up, and I would look around my room, listen for my sister's breath as she slept on the bunk bed below me, wonder where my mom was, what she was doing. I would lie there in the dark, the objects in the room changing shape in front of me, the noises of the neighborhood folding into themselvess until there was nothing but my sister's breathing, my own breathing, and it was then that I would rest.

Mom had a new home, an apartment, really. On our first visit, I sat cross-legged on dark brown carpeting, my back against a wall next to a skinny Christmas tree whose multi-colored lights lit the otherwise darkened room. Heavy curtains covered the few windows in the room. I tried to keep my brother quiet by playing a game of Candyland. Across the small room, a shirtless man slept on the couch under a frayed blanket. Mom was in the kitchen, and I could hear the sound of a Brillo pad scrubbing the inside of the ceramic sink, a pot roast baking in the oven with potatoes and carrots. Michael and I took turns making our way through King Kandy's kingdom of red, green, blue, yellow, orange, and purple square spaces. When he tried for the third time to get unstuck from landing on a black dot, he stomped his foot and kicked the board, sending cards and pieces in all different directions.

"I hate this game! I never win." He flipped the game board closed and crossed his arms.

The man on the couch stirred and sat up, letting the blanket fall around him, revealing the reddened grooves left in his back by the ridges in the couch cushions.

My mom came out of the kitchen and looked from Cliff to Michael, back to Cliff, waiting for a reaction, waiting for something. She rubbed her hands dry on the dish towel slung over her shoulder and said, "Sorry. I told them to be quiet." She looked at my brother and me and lowered her voice, "Pick that up! Your grandparents will be here soon. If you leave a mess, they won't give you any presents."

Cliff grumbled, scratched his beard, then walked to the back of the apartment, and slammed the bedroom door.

I followed my mom into the kitchen, leaving Michael to fling Candyland cards around the room until my sister laughed and joined in on the fun.

"I'm thirsty," I said. "Can I have some milk?"

She shook her head and went back to the sink. "We don't have milk."

I looked in the fridge anyway, and saw there was little besides canned beer, an opened package of lunch meat, and a few Tupperware containers concealing leftovers.

"Here," she said and filled a small glass with water from the faucet, "Have some water."

I sat at the small metal table and took the glass from her.

"It's cloudy," I said as I watched a white film swirl in the water.

"It just needs to settle. You can drink it."

I didn't know what that meant, so I waited until the water appeared clear before putting the edge of the glass to my lips and sipping slowly.

In the summer, I grew accustomed to the sounds of distant lawn mowers, baby birds chirping from an unseen nest high in the trees, bees circling my head on their way to the next dandelion. By

August everything around was so quiet I could almost hear the air getting thicker. Then the rains came, followed by the imminent threats of tornado warnings that flashed across the bottom of the television screen.

After we changed into pajamas, my brother and I would sit on the floor in the living room and try to ignore the snowy picture that the antenna just couldn't fix. He would nudge me every time another county would change color on the state map in the corner of the TV and ask me if that mean the tornado was coming for us. Outside, the wind would blow harder as the sky got darker; it would get under the siding of our trailer and howl throughout the living room. Lights would flicker. The tree in our yard would shake. Then the rain would fall, harder and harder, and we'd listen for any sign that it was getting worse, until we had to go to bed.

Once we were in bed, we thought we were safe, but there were many nights that year when my dad woke us up and made us hunker down in the hallway because it was the only space in our trailer that didn't have a window. I had learned how to do tornado drills in school, so I coached my brother. Face the wall. Knees tucked in and head tucked under. This was to protect us from flying shards of glass and other bits of destruction. Don't talk. I never fully understood how silence was going to protect us, but we shut up anyway. I usually spent those tornado drills watching the ants crawl across the floor, or counting the number of dots in the speckled tile, all the while grateful that I had gotten out of math class.

At home, it was a different kind of fear. We brought our pillows and blankets into the hallway, sat on the floor and stared at each other, our eyes wide, our mouths closed, and our ears tuned in to the wind crashing up against the side of our trailer, howling, howling, the sky too dark to warn us if the tornado was on its way.

The next day, my friends and I would cruise around on our bikes to look for the sheets of skirting that we had lost during the storm. The skirting were simply large slabs of metal that matched the siding, and their edges were sharp. They slid on a track underneath the house, and when it got windy enough, the edges would be caught just right that they would pull away from the house and collect with tree limbs, discarded toys, other debris.

The slabs of skirting were heavy, big and awkward and we could usually only balance one at a time on our handlebars, and even then it was wobbly and slow-going. There were usually quite a few neighbors out looking for their own skirting, and sometimes we brought back slabs that didn't belong to us, sometimes someone else took our slab when it didn't belong to them.

It was the third summer that I had collected skirting from throughout the mobile home park, but it was the first summer that I had done so without my mom asking. We hadn't seen her since Christmas, since that quick gift exchange with my grandparents. Sometimes she would call during the day when I was out riding with my friends, but Pam never told me. I wouldn't know until she would call again and say she had been trying and trying to reach us, that she was coming to get us soon because she was getting a new place, a house that was big enough for all of us. Sometimes I would try to call her, though it had to be quick or in secret because it was long distance. Sometimes, though, it didn't matter because the number would no longer be in service.

I pedaled through puddles along the sidewalk, puddles that would ride up my back bike tire and leave a spotted trail down my spine and all over the seat of my paints. The trail stained itself into my clothes, clothes that I didn't have very many of, and rarely saw new ones.

Worms always came out after those storms and would stretch themselves long and skinny across the sidewalk. It didn't smell refreshing after those storms. It smelled like death and rot. I'd aim my bike tire at those worms and run them over. I'd feel especially pleased if my tire severed them, as if it were some kind of retribution for the gashes on my hands from the skirting's sharp edges. Anything, everything, can cut something else.

Mom was taking us to a new place for the weekend. She called it Candyland. All of the streets were named after some type of treat: Fudge, Chocolate, Vanilla, and Butternut. Turn a corner and drive along Spearmint or Peppermint, or Wintergreen, or Ginger. Venture down Pecan, Almond, or Cashew, or cruise over to the fruit loop: Pear, Apple, Cherry, Lemon, and Orange. I whispered the name of each street aloud, as I heard the click of the lighter and smelled the menthol cigarette smoke as it filled the tiny car.

Mom's car didn't have air conditioning, so we rode with the windows down. The hot air blew into the car and circulated with mom's cigarette smoke. My hair stuck to my sweaty neck, and I squirmed on the fabric seat covered in burn holes, which would accumulate over time when flicked ash wouldn't quite make it out the window.

Despite the street names, Candyland was anything but magical. Trailers lined the curved, two-lane roads that snaked throughout the community. Each trailer—or mobile home, as Mom would correct me—had a single-car driveway, and many had a shed in the yard, near the back. There wasn't much else.

I watched the street names change with each turn as the roads curved and snaked along freshly cut grass and white sidewalks. Gum Drop, Licorice, Marshmallow, and—finally— Lollipop Lane, where mom pulled her car into a driveway and parked it in front of a powder blue, single-wide trailer.

"We're here," she announced. My brother and sister gathered their backpacks and duffle bags and scrambled out of the car. I took my time unbuckling my seatbelt and opening the door. I stared at the trailer that stood before me. The front door was on the side of the house and entered into a narrow living room. There were two bedrooms—the one all the way in the front where my sister and I shared a queen-sized bed, and mom's room in the back. My brother got the couch, and by default, the TV that he would watch all night, the blue light from the flickering screen flashing under my doorway, a light that would wake me up throughout the night. I would seethe with jealousy when bedtime came.

Mom had an obsession with cleanliness, but she always seemed to miss the mark on organization and decorating. She accessorized rooms in themes—geese in the kitchen, gold-plated sconces hanging on the walls in the living room, something pink in the bathroom, a lot of brown, and a lot of blue. Cheap prints in matching gold frames hung in jagged rows, potpourri in ceramic dishes adorning the worn and scratched end tables.

There was always a certain level of homogeny in mom's homes—the plain ivory walls, yellowed and aged vertical blinds, worn carpeting, all decorating features of a rental, a temporary home place. A keen eye could identify the settling cracks as they peeked out from behind the print of a washed out landscape. This home was no different. It bore no resemblance to the sweet and colorful pathways through Candyland. There was no Candy Cane Forest or Gum Drop Mountain.

Mom's Candyland didn't last long. Like the board game itself, the time spent there was transitory. No sooner would she update her bathroom with matching towels and a shower curtain, would the unpaid rent catch up with her, and she would disappear from our lives until she was settled someplace new and felt more prepared to be a mom—our mom. But for her, motherhood was not a love story, a match made in heaven, a Hollywood cliché, or an inspiration for others to emulate. For her, it was something she had to keep up with, and she fell behind in parenting as often as she fell behind in paying the rent. Yet, even as I grew older and realized motherhood was not her true calling, it didn't stop me from hoping for her phone calls or staring out the window while waiting for her car on visitation weekends. Her mothering couldn't, and didn't, stop me from trying to be her daughter.

36.
Of Overtime and the Beginning
Michael D. Jones

Once the beginning began, Overtime
Which is both within and beyond all time
Invisibly stirred among the cooling stars
Like dark matter adding weight to the Universe
(As if Time's slow tick didn't weigh enough)
So when Time first smiled and crawled
For the camera, Overtime leaned waiting
The patient twin unseen against the outer edge.
And when Time first cried out in the void
Overtime moved with compassion, answered
Whaaaa... with *...ahhhh* in the near distance
(Overtime never echoes and always answers).
So when the Creator first willed the darkness
Into light, and brought forth rules for the game
Time and Overtime had already doped it out-
Time, in all its authority and majestic splendor
Would have its day, and Overtime all the rest
(Which is both within and beyond all time
Over time); the beginning began once
With stirring breath, divining spark, weight.

37.
Offering Living Water
Carmanie Bhatti

I will remain blessed
when I will inherit my
God's kingdom prepared !

The Lord will teach me
to give food and drink to those
who hunger and thirst

That is how I'll be
offering Living Water
In a dry, bare land

For some need a hand,
Some healing of wounds which is
By prayer, service

There are many who
Are in travail, death, mourning,
Turmoil, suffering

I will keep my eyes
Open and ears attentive ,
To hear, see their pain !

I will remember
all the days of my life to
take care of the "least"

I will humbly bow
to my Lord God, who took care
of me, a stranger

Those of my brothers
and sisters who were scattered,
will be fed by God

The Lord will be a
shepherd, one who will seek
the lost sheep of the fold

Will the people of
God no longer be strayed, but
have eternal life !

38.
One More for the Road
Heath Bowen

The old man had miles of highway
dust on his shoes and Kentucky bourbon
on his breath when he blew in from
New Orleans. The valley wind hummed

river tunes as the barge horn blew
in from the bank. His thin strings of hair
hidden under a charcoal colored porkpie
given to him by a juke joint

owner just outside of Mississippi.
This was long before the rain came
and the cobblestones were covered
by lake house debris and an underwater

fusion of tainted fish. He first came into my diner
after I purchased it from the Warrens
at auction. I offered him honest pay,
but he only wanted coffee.

I saw him last a month ago.
I was facing West; facing the sun
as it fell below the Sycamore tree.
His nicotine teeth snuck through a wounded smile,

both shoes still covered from the country road
he's traveled. Today, when I look out the window,
the sidewalk is empty, dusty, devoid of fish and ruin
and the old man with the brass band at his back.

39.
Overtime and the Dance
Michael D. Jones

Overtime no longer maintains control, the crowd
In its frenzy of immediacy and spontaneous
Combustibility, excites the air   the walls   the space
Between the air and walls, excites *thumpa-thumpa*
Emerging rhythm, unaware that space now breathes
The bodies on their feet as they reach and reach.
Thumpa-thumpa, thumpa-thumpa. The heart translates
Overtime's singular thought underlying all thought
Thumpa-thumpa: here, not-here; limited, delimited
Over time, over-what; and in the ecstasy of the eternal
Present- Overtime *(unaware in the moment of itself)*
Left the house, curling iron on, front door wide open
Wandering among the masses gathered in the street
Both of and beyond time- becomes self-forgetful.
Space no longer exists; everything holds together
From pure desire for harmony.   Time and Overtime
Reconcile, expanding the scope of whatever happens
In a perfected atmosphere.   *Thumpa-thumpa*, the crowd
Like so many tenuous atoms held together then torn
Apart and recombined by an unseen force, realigns
Forming more stable structures, stronger relationships
Thumpa-thumpa, the timeless beat pulses and thrums.
The crowd no longer maintains control over time.

40.
Overtime
Earl W. Wolfe

First

I went and got some coffee and talked business with the guys,
We got into an argument.   Their golf scores were all lies!
I left and got some folders from the vacation flier rack,
And went into the men's room and read them front to back.
I was lucky 'cause the stall had both the Free Press and the News.
I read them, did both crosswords, then took a little snooze.
Now it's getting close to quitting time, so back to work I'll creep,
But disaster struck!   I can't stand up!   Both legs have gone to sleep!

Second

Here I am in the men's room,
I'm sitting on the pot.
I'm really sick, I'm terribly weak
My forehead's awfully hot.
I've diarrhea, I'm vomiting,
I think that I might die.
I don't know if I'll make it home,
Although I'm going to try.
I've got to last out three more hours
It is a rotten crime,
But it's better here than back at home,
'Cause Sundays we get double time!

Third

Every time the boss comes by, I'm busier than Hell,
He often pats me on the back; says I'm doing well.
I never walk, I always trot, never listen for the bell.
I'm extremely, awfully busy: everyone can tell.
This lousy job has got me down, my back is awfully sore.
I've done the same thing sixteen times, undone it even more.
The way I have to stretch my day is certainly a crime,
But that's the only way I know of – to justify overtime.

41.
Pavement Ends
Chase Pielak

Where the pavement ends
Is a very scary place

Gravel has popped tires.
It flies unexpectedly, dangerous.

And the compass and the charts
Cannot lead the way...

But perhaps it is the way home -
To adventure and safety
Never before possible.

42.
Pie
Mark Hudson

When the doors shut, and the footsteps died,
a couple of kids were caught sneaking pie.
Their mom came in with a broom in her hand,
and on their butts the broom did land.
Both of the children wailed in disbelief,
Cursing their luck, for both being thieves.
The pie was on their thumbs and their fingers,
and on their butts, the pain really lingered.
The kids raced for the bedroom to hide,
the pies were out on the table open wide.
The mother was sad her children misbehaved,
The pie was something she'd hoped she could save.
But now the counter is full of cherries,
and some of the crumbs were hidden and buried.
The mother sighs, thoroughly annoyed,
seeing the pie that her children destroyed.
She paused to reflect and studied the pies,
then scooped out a sliver that tempted her eyes.
The pies were meant for her children to eat,
but now she nibbles on the pie so sweet.
And then she realizes the kids are sweet, too,
she feels bad that she hit them with a broom.
She takes the rest of the pie to their room,
to make amends to the kids from her womb.

43.
Poem for the People of God
(who think they are physically disabled)
Carmanie Bhatti

The Creator said
"Let there be light, and there was "light,"
the light with tones and hues

I am part of that light,
with my own color,
and impression, beauty

None can challenge me,
nor refute the composition
of this art created by God

None can be like me,
for God made me unique
with a distinct flavor

None can spill me, nor can waste me,
none can refill me,
but God alone

None can weaken me,
for I am the work of God's hands,
made to live as only I can

This art has many colors in it,
I am one of them;
color distinct

I am proud to be
a colorful piece of this art
created by God, perfect!

44.
Prayer Based on John 4
Carmanie Bhatti

May we walk on roads
Where sinners dwell, who are the
Wells without water

May we hesitate
Not, to converse with those who
Wait for a question

May our eyes see poor,
The marginalized around
Us, as Jesus did

May we become tired
To rest near wells to help the
Thirsty souls quench thirst

May the wells inside
Us have water for all to
Give life eternal

May we forget not
To be thirsty for thirsty,
Weak, abandoned souls

May our words have the
Power to make other wells
The gushing waters

May we say Amen
To feed hungry with word
To give life from death

45.
Prayer Quilt
Mark Hudson

A bunch of women from my mother's church built
a healing gift for her cancer, a prayer quilt.
The quilt hung from the church for weeks,
people added threads so the spirit could speak.
People would tie a knot on the string,
and up above the angels would sing.
The cancer was healed, and God was praised,
and everybody who prayed was amazed.
From Florida, they sent the quilt to mother,
it was hung on her wall like a giant cover.
It showed that God's arms cover us all,
the quilt symbolized God's love on the wall.
But now in Florida while on vacation,
The cancer came back to all our frustration.
The quilt seemed like an answer to prayer,
but now I can show my mom that I care.
The cancer returning is bad news,
it's the reason I feel such blues.
My mom will have to take chemo once more,
so the quilt is something I do not adore.
I hope my mother receives God's will,
that she'll go to heaven if she's really ill.
But either way I'll be here on Earth,
it's hard to feel too much mirth.
If it's my mama's time to go,
I hope she knows I love her so.

*(Updated note; my mother did pass away from cancer about
a year ago. The prayer quilt is still up in the condo where
my father stays in the summer. It is a good reminder of her,
and that she is in a better place. This poem is dedicated to her.)*

46.
Round Trip
Michael D. Jones

Part One: GRR to Palm Coast

For eight long minutes you made me forget.
Yes, inches of early dark lake effect snow
Left me in 32B while runway plows cleared
And the self-absorbed fumed their poison
Let me off now's and *I don't care about's*
For over two hours, you have no idea my
Beloved massage chair how demeaning
(Demean: Latin; drive animals) yes, demeaning
Flying coach in Winter is; being packed in
Jostled, stifled, and compressed. Yes, you
Made me forget I missed my connection
In Cincinnati where air marshals arrested
Some hooded punk outside my gate. Yes
You squeezed my cramped Seat E memories
Of XXL brothers who thought I'd move. Yes
You chopped away my second flight delay
Waiting on a new part for the cockpit. Yes
You effleuraged my re-route in Atlanta
After missing a second Jacksonville flight
Which by this point I almost did not mind-
Why not Daytona in November en route
To Palm Coast? It is half an hour closer
To my aged Eighty-Seven year old father
Who no longer travels or says, *Yes*. You
Were set in Concourse F just for me; yes
Destined to meet on my return flight. Yes
You kneaded my tired calves, knees, thighs
My gluteus, *oh*, rocked my aching hips, *oh*,
Firmly rolled your way up my back. Oh, yes
My massage chair, like a snake charmer you
Relaxed muscle groups and aligned my spine
Cleared my mind; *Yes,* I give you, *Thanks.*
I tingled after the vibrations stopped, walking
To my next gate. The best dollar I ever spent.

Part 2: Ode to a Massage Chair, Concourse F
Minneapolis-St. Paul International Airport

For eight minutes you made me forget.
Yes,

                   , you

                        , yes,
                   ;
                            . Yes, you

                                . Yes
You
                                   . Yes
You
                             . Yes
You

                               .

               ?

                      , *Yes*. You
                           ; yes.
                       . Yes
You
         , *oh,*   , *oh,*
                      . Oh, yes
                         you

          ; *Yes,*   you, *Thanks.*

   . Yes, the best dollar I ever spent.

47.
School Dummy
Sarah Z. Sleeper

Colin walked down to the end of the dock and dove off, slapped to hyper-alertness by the brisk tingle of fresh cold spring water, his pale freckled face instantly pink. He inhaled Walloon Lake's invigorating pine and birch odor, mingled with its oddly pleasant fishy scent. He dove below the rolling surface, forced the air out of his lungs in a bubbly rush. He surfaced, breathed, turned his face down. Two miles to the other side. He kicked fast and cupped handfuls of water, pushing them behind him, arms rotating around his shoulders in a slightly lopsided rhythm, "Crooked Rook," Betsy called it. His right arm, stronger than the left, completed each stroke a second faster. He compensated for this by kicking harder with his left leg, thigh muscles firm, slicing through the soft resisting lake water. Every two arm cycles, he turned his face to the side and swallowed a deep breath of cool air, saw a flash of sparkling blue sky. Just three weeks until the triathlon, his first in the over-forty age category. His segment times had been slipping, and he was determined to cut at least three minutes off the swim. He could not afford to miss any workouts in the next twenty-one days.

"You'll miss Adam's game if you do the lake swim. You're gonna get killed by a boat one of these days." The last thing Betsy had said to him as he walked down the steep stone pathway to the dock. He looked back to see her standing in the doorway, hand on her hip.

Colin lifted his head out of the water and looked toward the shore, now about half a mile ahead. A white Sea Ray roared past about twenty yards in front of him and the wake cascaded into his face, bobbing him up and down. He wondered if they had seen him. Without Betsy along on his swims, he had been making sure to wave his arms when he heard a boat in the vicinity, but he hadn't heard this one until it was right in front of him. He filled his lungs and began swimming again, went just close enough to the shore to touch his toe on the sandy bottom, then turned around to swim the two miles back.

"Dad, watch out for Nessie!" It's what Adam said every day before his lake swims. And this very morning Adam told him that he wouldn't mind if Colin missed his game. "I know you have to practice, Dad. I get it. That's what athletes do. Never take the easy road, right?"

Betsy used to paddle along beside Colin when he swam the lake, blocking for powerboats that might not see him on its white-capping surface. She quit that routine when Adam's summer baseball schedule conflicted with Colin's training routine, and she pushed Colin to train at the Y's indoor pool instead of the lake since the Y took less time. Colin hated the pool, with its odor of urine disguised by chorine and only swam at the Y when forced to do so by bad weather. Lake swimming, with the constant push and pull of waves churned by strong West Arm winds, offered a better training effect. His lungs and muscles had to work harder, become more efficient and better conditioned than they could get by pool swimming. It was a principle Colin felt strongly about—never take the path of least resistance, always accept the hardest challenge. A philosophy that brought him success as a triathlete.

Half-way back to the dock, at the lake's deepest point—two hundred feet—Colin felt something brush his leg. A hard smooth something bumped into his shin. If he could have jumped straight up out of the water, he would have.

He thrust his face down into the lake with open eyes. It was clear water, so clean, he could swim with no goggles, eyes open underwater. The something moved down, its dark grey oblong form sinking out of view into water that melted from blue to charcoal to black as it got deeper. Colin shivered and shook the water from his eyes, reminded himself that the only fish with teeth in Walloon Lake were bass, perch, catfish and trout that never exceeded two feet in length, and they wanted as little to do with him as he with them. In Walloon the fish were small-lake versions of the species, not the large Great Lakes fish with jutting incisors and broad O-shaped jaws. Those fish were rumored to have contributed to the demise of the Edmund Fitzgerald and other lost ships, to have taken the lives of hoards of disappeared fishermen. This fish, or whatever it was that Colin felt and saw, was probably much smaller than he perceived it to be, its size distorted by the movements and reflections of the waves and the currents underneath the surface. He pushed from his mind the Loch Ness Monster newspaper clippings that Adam saved in a photo album. He sprinted toward the dock and his lungs ached.

The ninth inning was just beginning when Colin took a seat next to Betsy on the whitewashed bleacher. She didn't turn her head or say hello, just stared at the field, at Adam on first base. Colin leaned in to try to kiss her on the cheek and whispered. "C'mon. Forgive me. I almost got hit by a boat and eaten by a shark. You're right. It's not safe out there." She slid down the bench away from him, then stood and cheered for Adam. When the game was over, Adam ran to them, punched Colin on the arm. "No homerun, Dad. Sorry." His tan face was dotted with dirt, his blue-and-white striped uniform dusted with red clay.

"Looked like a good game from what I saw. You won, so that's the point. Hey, and I shaved two minutes off my time." Betsy shot him a hard glance.

"That's great, Dad. You rock." Adam squinted in the slanting afternoon sun. "Mom, the guys asked me to go to Murdock's for ice cream. I dunno, though. I think I'd rather fish."

"You can do whatever you like Adam. I'll pick you up later if you want to walk over to Murdock's with them." Adam pushed the dirt around with his toe.

"Dad, you want to fish with me? The lake's supposed to be calm today." Adam didn't look up when he spoke, continued to trace lines in the dirt with his shoe. Betsy leveled her gaze at Colin, dropped her chin.

"Uh, sure Adam. I can fish for a little while."

"Usually you don't want to," Adam said, looking at his mother. Colin saw that his son was silently commiserating with her. She gave Adam a sympathetic look, something she hadn't turned Colin's way in months.

"Actually, Dad, you fish with me once out of every fourteen times I ask. I did the math."

Now Betsy looked at Colin with a combination of amusement and disdain.

"Is it that bad, Adam? Really?" Colin patted Adam on the shoulder and turned to walk to the car. "C'mon. Let's do it. Let's fish."

"Only if you really want to," Adam said, starting toward the car.

Betsy took Adam in her car and Colin followed them back to the cabin in his. He wondered if that was sarcasm he had just heard in his son's voice and wondered if ten was the age when kids started to become smart asses. As he drove, he puzzled over Adam's love of fishing. Why was his son drawn to such a quiet, solitary and non-athletic activity? It was an old-school, old-soul way to spend his time, so unusual for a kid his age. Yet Adam often chose it over anything else, and without fail, he invited Colin to join him. When Colin did go along, he had marveled at his son's skill and knowledge. Adam knew that the green and silver shimmering fly would attract trout, and that bass went for the white fuzzy one. He knew the best fishing spots, the coves where catfish gathered to feed, and what sandbars and deep drop-offs attracted trout. He showed Colin where the lake's shallow spots were, where to steer the Chris Craft to avoid unmarked narrows, where the water was smoothest for skiing, and which were the sunniest and most beautiful picnic spots. Colin knew the lake from his physical battles with it. Adam knew it from studying it, spending time with it, befriending it.

Back at the cottage, Adam ran inside, grabbed one of his rods, and stood in the doorway. He looked so tall for a ten-year-old, framed in the rectangle of the sliding glass door, head almost hitting the metal top edge. Adam was burlier than Colin had been at that age and dark, like Betsy, with deep brown eyes and tawny skin. "Going down, Dad," he shouted over his shoulder, as he ran down the stone steps.

"Okay. I'll see you down there," Colin called, knowing even as he said it that he would keep it short so he could get his running miles in.

Colin found Betsy in the bedroom, sitting on the bench at the end of their bed, taking off her tennies. Her hair was messy and hung into her eyes, blown out of its tidy style by the wind at the baseball diamond. He wanted to kiss her, but knew she'd rebuff him. "Betsy, shit. My race is so soon. I can't afford to miss any workouts. I have to do the toughest, longest ones now, for at least two more weeks. You used to understand that."

She brushed her hair off her forehead and looked up at him, her face flat, unreadable. "What I understand is that you always put you first. Before me, before us, before Adam. Don't you see a problem with that?" She pursed her slender lips in anger, then exhaled heavily and wiped her eyes with the back of her hand. "No more lake swims. They take too long. I don't want Adam to watch you swim away from the cabin every day when you should be doing something with him. Go swim at the Y. That's it. Just go there."

Her tiny body slouched. She used to be a triathlete too and was sinewy from her years of training. If he hadn't seen her crush the competition in the Mackinaw Marathon fifteen years back, he would have passed her by, thought she was frail. That was the last thing she was.

"C'mon, Bets. You used to be part of it too. I think the problem is you don't support me."

"Me support you? What about you supporting Adam? I'm tired of carrying your load, compensating for your lack of effort."

"Lack of effort? Compensating? That's a low blow. I always try, always take the most difficult road."

"Being an athlete doesn't give you a pass to be a laggard as a dad. Adam already behaves like he's an accessory in your life. He automatically marginalizes himself because you've done it to him for so long. I won't stand by and watch my son's spirit being slowly deflated. I will NOT do it."

"Your son? Now he's your son? What do you want me to do, quit racing? Just quit after twenty years? What kind of a lesson would that teach Adam? That you quit things when they get difficult?"

Betsy stood, gave him a sad look. "Eat, train, sleep. That's it. That's all there is to you." She turned her back to him and walked into the bathroom.

Colin's gut jumped. He felt lightheaded, limbs devoid of muscle, filled up with helium, arms floating away from his body. He stood in place a good five minutes, breathing in, breathing out, nothing else. She'd been mad before, but never this upset. He cleared his throat, trying to think of what to say. Finally she came out of the bathroom, purse in hand.

"Betsy, after this race, I'll do better. I'll cut back on training. Okay?" Not the most convincing speech, but she paused midstride, studied his face.

"Yeah, right," she retorted. She dismissed him with a curt wave, brushed by him on her way out. "I'm going out on some errands. Don't you have a run you have to do now?"

He listened to the car crunching up the gravel driveway. He changed into his running clothes, walked zombie-like around their summer place. Wicker furniture, plastic lake-proof dishware, warm comforters to fend off the chilly Northern Michigan nights. Trophy fish—the two-foot-long kind with tiny harmless teeth—hung on the wall by the fireplace, mouths gaping, eyes glassed over. Colin would have removed them but Adam thought they were cool and insisted they stay. Strangely, though neither Betsy nor Colin fished, Adam had taken it up when he was five, fishing with anyone he could round up, joining the Walloon Fishermen's Club. Now at ten, he was an absolute devotee of rod and reel, had a full collection of aluminum and wood rods, colorful flies and lake lures, and kept them on display in the top compartments of his open tackle box right by the sliding glass door, ready any time the fish were biting.

Colin walked out onto the back patio, looked down the steep hill and saw Adam on the dock. He still had on his baseball uniform and wasn't fishing, just standing, facing the sparkling, glinting water, looking into the distance. The sun-and-cloud-washed summer sky was melting from bright blue into an orange, yellow and crimson sunset. He picked up Adam's tackle box and a rod. Maybe if he skipped today's run, Betsy would calm down.

"Still want to fish?" Adam jumped, hadn't heard Colin coming.

"Oh, Dad. You scared me."

"You look like you're in deep thought there, buster."

"Not really." Adam's dark eyes were glazed over as if in a reverie, but suddenly focused on his father. "Sure, let's fish." Adam took the rods and deftly attached to each a brown feathery lure with a red spot, he gave one to Colin. They plopped the lines into the water on the deep side of the dock. Always more likely to be fish lurking there in the shade, Adam had said.

"Your mom's on my case."

Adam shifted foot-to-foot, dragging the line back and forth through the water. "Why, because you don't come to my games?"

"Yes. That. She thinks I train too much instead of doing things with you, fishing, for instance."

"You don't like fishing. I know you're doing it now because you feel like you have to. I know you'd rather be running."

Colin was stung by the truth of Adam's statement. Adam hadn't met Colin's eyes since he'd come down to the dock. At that moment, Colin wanted more than anything for his son to look right into his face so he could search it and see if Betsy was right. He was the boy's father, after all. Shouldn't he be able to read his son?

"Dad, why do you run so much? No one else's father runs as much as you do." Adam's voice was soft, patiently inquiring, almost patronizing.

Colin felt like a child himself, fumbling for the right answer on a test. "For one thing, it helps pay the bills," he said, feeling silly.

"Other dads pay the bills without running." This time, Colin thought for sure Adam was being sarcastic. Adam pulled up his line and moved to the shallower side of the dock. Colin followed and they both plopped their lures in the water again.

"Well, yes. My day job would pay our bills. You're right." Colin drew a deep breath. "Okay, well, I guess I run because I like to run. It's my favorite thing to do." As soon as he said it, he realized it was the wrong thing, could be interpreted in several hurtful ways.

Adam stood still, no longer dragging the line, just dangling it below the surface. "Okay," he said. "I get it. Like I love fishing." He pulled up the line, replaced it a little to the south. "Only you can fish with me, but I can't run with you."

"Adam," Colin started, "I'll spend more time with you. As soon as this race is over." Colin's voice sounded hollow in his own ears. Adam didn't turn away from the lake, but Colin saw his mouth harden, like Betsy's had done earlier.

Adam's line jerked. He yanked up on it, sinking the hook deeper into his catch. He gripped the rod with both hands, braced himself on the dock with his feet. The fish had some fight in it, wasn't going to give up easily. Colin dropped his rod onto the dock and jumped behind Adam, put his arms around him, grabbed the rod with one hand and the reel with the other. Together, they strained and tugged and inched the line in. Neither spoke, they worked together like two parts of one machine, Adam leaning forward to create slack in the line, Colin turning the reel at just the right moment, a second before Adam stood upright again. They continued this swaying, inch-by-inch work, tugging, pulling and stepping back in unison, shortening the line to bring the catch closer and closer. Finally, the simultaneous snap of four arms and a great jolt propelled Adam and Colin two feet backward. The fish was up. In one deft motion Adam unhooked it and dropped it onto the dock, where it lay flapping and gasping. They stepped away from each other and stared at their catch.

"What is that, Dad?" Colin was so startled that he didn't register Adam's question.

"Geezus, Adam. What kind of fish is that?"

"I don't know. I've never seen one before." Adam ran over to the dock box, grabbed a net and put the fish in the holding box attached to the side of the dock. "That thing must be three feet long. Wow, Dad. Did you see those teeth? I've never seen a black fish before, only catfish are black. That's not a catfish. Did you see that bright blue scale on its side?"

Colin shuddered, remembering the thing that had brushed against his shin. "Let's take a picture. We can look it up online."

Staring down at the creature, now aggressively poking its nose this way and that into the thick wire netting of the holding box, Adam was silent. After a few seconds, he turned and looked at Colin full in the face, raised his eyebrows and broke open into a broad smile.

Upstairs Colin and Adam sat side-by-side at the dining room table, laptop open. They quickly found a photo of a similar fish. "Giant Asian Carp," the caption read. "Invasive species, accidentally introduced to the Mississippi River in 2000, slowly migrating north. Great Lakes geologists built a barrier in the Chicago River, an attempt to block the carp from entering Lake Michigan. The carp is a threat to the native species as well as to boaters."

"A threat to boaters? Like Moby Dick, a fish that breaks boats? Or like Jaws, a shark that eats people? Oh my God, Dad, if it's not in Lake Michigan, how did it get into Walloon? Can it bite us when we're swimming? We probably shouldn't eat it, right?"

"That's a lot of questions Adam. The truth is I don't know the answer to any of them."

"We better tell somebody, right?"

"I guess you better. I'll help you, but I think you should do it. After all, you caught it." Colin felt a twinge of guilt about his scheduled run, but was genuinely enjoying the immersion in the fish detective work with his son. "Maybe look up the Michigan Fish and

Game department or something like that. Google that."

They spent the next two hours online, reading more about the carp, sending e-mails to people they hoped were the proper authorities, even to the editor of the Graphic Resorter, the small local newspaper. Each note was signed by Adam. "Thank you for your consideration. Sincerely, Adam Lee." When Betsy came home they were still sitting there. The cabin was dark except for the dining room's overhead lamp and the light from the computer screen.

"Well, what are you two up to? I expected you to be running."

"Mom! You'll never guess what we caught! It's an Asian Carp and it's not even supposed to be in Walloon. It has huge teeth and eats other fish. It also flies into people's faces and hurts them! C'mon down to the dock and I'll show you." Adam stood and grabbed Betsy's arm.

"No, no. Not now Adam. It's too dark and the path lights aren't working. Can't I look at it tomorrow? And what do you mean it flies into people's faces?"

"When a boat's engine scares it, it jumps out of the water and sometimes it hits people in the face. It might bite them too, we're not sure." Colin smiled, enjoying the way when Adam called them "we."

Betsy glared at Colin. "What about the run? Aren't you supposed to be in training?" Definite sarcasm.

"I didn't go. Didn't even realize how freezing it is until just now either." He went to the bedroom to put on sweats over his running shorts. Betsy followed.

"So, you've been here with Adam for the past three hours? Fishing?"

"It was sort of an accident. After you left I wandered down to the dock and this is what happened. We discovered a fish. I don't think I've ever seen Adam this excited."

He thought he caught a hint of a smile from her, the first almost-friendly face he'd seen from her in months.

In the morning, dark clouds loomed over the lake, thunder boomed a few miles away. Janice Mechum, the editor of the local paper, came over at ten, along with a photographer. Adam led them down to the dock, Colin and Betsy followed. When Adam lifted the heavy wood lid to reveal his catch the holding box was empty. There was a jagged hole in the wire netting. The carp had bashed or chewed through it. Adam looked stricken, his mouth twisted sideways. Colin put an arm around his son's shoulders. "Adam, it's okay."

The editor chimed in. "Yes, it's fine Adam. We still want the story." She wiped small drops of drizzle from her glasses and they went upstairs, just making it inside as the sky opened up. She interviewed Adam and he showed her the photo he had taken. Colin kept his distance, listened in from the kitchen.

"I have never seen a fish like this, ever," he heard Adam say. "And I've been fishing here for years." Colin smiled to himself, impressed with the authority in his son's voice.

"That's a doozy alright," the editor said. "Adam, I can't thank you enough for contacting us. This story is going be big. Thank you so much."

"I'm going to catch it again. I swear I will. Right, Dad?" Adam turned toward the kitchen, waved his father over. "Actually, my dad caught it with me. Make sure you put that in the story too, okay?"

Colin didn't take his lake swim that day, not safe to swim when there's lightening, he told Adam, who replied, "Duh." He didn't do the Y swim that day either, told Betsy that when the weather cleared he planned to help Adam find that fish again. The day passed without a break in the downpour. They started a fire, made popcorn, watched Jurassic Park for the third time. "Dinosaurs evolved from fish," Adam said, pointing to the screen. "Did you know that, Dad? Four hundred million years ago, creatures called tetrapods crawled out of the water and started morphing into dinosaurs. Isn't that amazing?" Colin had no response, just stared at his son.

"Adam, your dad isn't as smart as you," Betsy said, her head poking out from her blanket on the end of the couch, a wry smile on her lips. "Keep that in mind when you tell him stuff."

Colin ran and biked just five days of the next two weeks. He spent hours each day helping Adam in his quest to recapture the carp. They rowed or motored, morning and evening to different spots on the lake, looking for shady shallows where the carp could be hiding. Adam used the same brown feather lure every day. When the paper came out, Adam was a minor celebrity at his Tuesday afternoon baseball game. The Detroit Free Press called, and so did television reporters from three stations. Walloon Lake was descended on by fishermen and fisherwomen of all sorts, trying to catch the carp or its relative. Swimmers, usually teeming in Walloon Lake, became scarce, unsure if the carp would bite, worried there were more. The frenzy of fishing went on for the rest of the summer.

It was Adam who caught the carp again, right off the dock and right in the same spot, thirteen days after the first catch. Again, Colin helped him haul in the beast and deposit it into the newly installed thick aluminum holding box. The photo comparison confirmed that it was indeed the same carp, same blue spot on the side, not a typical all-black one. An official from the Fish and Game Department came and took it away for study.

Re-catching the carp didn't dampen Adam's passion. He fished every day, off the dock, in shallow water with waders on his legs and using a fly rod, out alone in the rowboat, or with Colin along to drive the Chris Craft. He caught schools of perch and bass that Betsy and Colin helped him cook up for dinners.

"I'd really like to catch another big one," Adam said, spooning rainbow sherbet into his mouth. "Maybe you're the reason I caught the carp, Dad. Maybe you brought me good luck."

"I'm pretty sure I don't deserve that much credit, Adam."

"Well, I couldn't have hauled it in without you."

Betsy looked at Adam, and her eyes were bluer than the shimmering lake behind her. When she picked up the dessert bowls, he thought he felt her arm brush his shoulder.

No other carp were ever found in Walloon Lake. No one had a good explanation for how that one had gotten there. Rumors abounded—Someone planted it there to wreck the pristine lake. One of the big sailboats had accidentally carried it in, hiding in its bait box. It wasn't a carp at all, just a mutant catfish. After a month or so the carp buzz died off, swimmers returned.

Colin did the triathlon and placed fiftieth, his poorest finish ever. Betsy met him at the end with a bottle of water and a warm kiss, the best he could remember. Adam had his carp photo framed and hung it with the other ugly trophies near the fireplace. Colin shuddered every time he looked at that photo. He couldn't shake the heebie jeebies he felt remembering the heavy thump on his shin. Like most people, he believed that there were no other carp in Walloon Lake, but still, he lost his taste for lake swimming. His drive to run and bike tapered off too. He felt the training urge wane, like the pleasant drifting of mental acuity after a cocktail or two; and he had been joining Betsy on the patio most nights to sip wine in the sunset. He thought maybe he'd take a pass on the next race, take Adam and Betsy to Mackinaw Island for the weekend instead.

Colin thought about the carp too. He never found out how that fish made it all the way to Walloon, but Adam had a theory that seemed better than most. The carp was the dummy of his school. While all the other carps stayed south in friendlier waters and more moderate climates, this one stubborn fish had to try things the hard way. He was compelled to swim upstream, upcurrent, moving north into colder, less-hospitable lakes. Adam and Colin had done the carp a favor by catching it, because as the cool Northern Michigan end of summer becomes the cold autumn and then the frigid winter, the carp, unable to find its way back downstream, would have surely perished there in Walloon Lake, alone.

48.
Shopping with My Wife
John Grey

I'm bored with sitting
in what I always refer to
as "the men's chair"
If it really was a men's chair.
it would come with copies
of Sports Illustrated or Soldier of Fortune
or Auto Magazine.

But it's either this
or move about the store
and run the risk
of some middle aged woman
tapping me on the shoulder,
to ask. "Can I help you?"

I gravitate to the chair
for that very reason.
I don't want to be associated
with sale items on racks,
accessories.
long glittery gowns with
tight-end shoulder pads,
black netting overskirts,
proper gray suits
for the up-and-coming
businesswoman.

I am the swan
amid ducklings.
the childless in a conversation
with proud fathers of newborns.
I am here
but I am not here.
My wife is in the dressing room
trying on six outfits.
Anonymity, invisibility -
both fit me.

49.
Sparky
Mark Hudson

Inspired by a true story from a local newspaper in Florida a few years ago.

Everett Mack is ninety-six,
spent his life doing magic tricks.
This man from Florida played a clown,
in Silver Lakes, that was the town.
He played "Sparky" a role that inspired,
now the man has chosen to retire.
Mack, a shiner for sixty years,
retired and left people shedding tears.
He came to Naples to join a band,
playing bagpipes he hoped to be grand.
But he found no solace in this endeavor,
he found as a clown he was rather clever.
He has been to Philadelphia and Boston,
and Miami clowning in costume.
On the streets he carried balloons,
he looks like a character from cartoons.
His grandchildren love his creations, too,
for a senior citizen, he never feels blue.
But now he must retire and it's known,
"Sparky" is gone but Everett is grown.
A real clown never really retires,
his act matures and continues to inspire.

50.
Sultry Goodbyes
Deborah Guzzi

In late August the torrid air drifts on the lake.
The sky glowers, striking a contrast, black to gray.
Soon, very soon, the lake with be thundered awake;
the mirage waver, then, dissolve in disarray.

The last of children's giggles now echo ghostly
past the woods at water's edge mixed with robin song.
Pink skinned lover's necking will be a memory
and their cuddling shooed indoors where it belongs.

The vegetables gone, each lettuce plant has yielded
scorched by the heat. Fields and forest long for autumn,
but praise the heat of summer which raised the corn fields,
lift a glass from the gift of the apple and the plum.

Say goodbye to August with a gentle kiss on the breeze
for the wild geese are flying through the changing trees.

51.
The Boy Beneath the Beech Tree
Edward Ahern

Once, not so long ago, a young boy lived with his grandmother in the woods outside a small town. His mother and father were gone, and his grandma was his only family.

His grandma was old, confused and forgetful, so David helped her to buy food, cook meals, and clean up their small house. David was still small, but loved his grandma and worked hard to make her comfortable.

Now, just outside the house and overshadowing it was a large, old beech tree with gnarly branches and roots. The beech tree was already old when grandma's house was built, and living under the tree, in its roots, was an old, gnarly troll, even older than the tree.

The troll, whose name was Plumblump, watched from the tree every day as the boy cleaned and washed and chopped wood. *I need a boy like this*, he thought, *to take care of me.*

Plumblump looked around at his cave under the tree. Roots grew here and everywhere, running up and down and criss and cross so he had to crawl between roots from one part of his cave to another. And Plumblump had short stubby legs and a thick belly, which made crawling around very clumsy.

"This boy could work for me, cleaning up the old bones and digging dirt from around the roots so I could walk around. By Lardilummox, I think I'll kidnap him."

And so Plumblump began paying close attention to what was happening in the grandma's house, sneaking out at night to look in the windows and listen to David and his grandma.

One night, after David had cooked the dinner and washed the dishes, grandma took his hand and said, "David, I must visit my sister Desdemona, because she is depressed. There is no room for you at her house. But do not worry, I will ask the Franklin family to take you in for a week while I am away."

And one day a wagon came to take grandma away for her visit. "Don't worry David," she said, "The Franklin father will be coming by later to pick you up." And off she went in the wagon.

But grandma, as she often was, was confused. She had forgotten to ask the Franklin family if David could stay with them, and so the Franklin father would not be coming.

That afternoon David chopped more wood and washed the clothes so that grandma would have clean clothes when she returned. When darkness came and the Franklin father had not arrived David was not afraid. *Grandma was confused,* he thought, *the Franklin father will probably come tomorrow.*

But Plumblump had been waiting for his chance to pounce. David and his grandma never locked their front door, and after David cooked his meal and washed his dishes and went to bed Plumblump simply walked in, grabbed David by one arm and his hair, dragged him out of the house and down into the cave under the beech tree.

David struggled, but the troll was really strong, so strong he could bend bones and break them. And David was more scared than he'd ever been before, for Plumblump was unusually ugly, even for a troll. He had warts on his face bigger than David's thumbs. His teeth were pond scum green and chipped from chewing on bones. His hands were as gnarled as beech roots, with curved claws.

"My grandma will be coming after me," David yelled.

Plumblump had not talked to anyone for three times David's age, so he hissed when he spoke. "Your grandmother is ssso confussssed ssshe'll think you wandered off and got lost in the woods. Poor little lost boy, ssshe'll never find you. And by Lardilummox I swear I'll make a good slave of you."

Plumblump put an iron collar around David's neck and locked it with a key. The collar was attached to a thick iron chain, which was bolted into the thickest part of the tree.

"You are my ssslave ssson. You will clean out the bones of animals and people. You will ssshovel wider openings for me to walk around in my cave. You will be fed roots and mushrooms and worms. And if you do not work as I wisssh your bonesss will be added to those on the floor."

David began to cry. Who would help him? Who would take care of his grandma?

"You can cry asss you work," Plumblump said," crying isss sssoothing to me."

And so for three days David cleaned the bones, broken and whole out of the cave. After dark, Plumblump showed him a bog in which to put the bones. And for two more days David dug wider walkways so the troll's fat belly could bumble through the cave.

On the sixth day, the day before grandma was due back, David was still digging.

"Who will watch over grandma," he thought. "She only has me and I only have her."

And just then his spade sliced into a skunk burrow. The skunk father and mother hissed at him worse even than the troll's hiss. But they did not spray their skunk stink at him. For the troll ate almost any animal and thought that skunk smell was sweet. If the troll smelled skunk he himself would dig until he discovered and ate them.

So the skunks just stared and hissed at David, until the father skunk waddled his way up to David and looked him closely in the face.

Now, everybody knows that skunks can't talk. But when they're awfully anxious they can convey broken bits of thoughts.

"Boy. Boy! You dirt back put. Troll us from save."

David, scared and shocked, said nothing.

"Boy. Boy! Coming troll soon. Us help must you."

And the skunk noticed the collar closed around David's neck and the chain clanking behind him.

"Boy. Boy! Ah. Protect us you, Free way get to you tell."

David thought he understood. He began to talk to the skunk and in his skunkish style the father skunk thought back. And amazingly they agreed.

David dumped the dirt back over the skunk burrow, and covered it over with rootlets and rubbish. Then, when he next went out with a bucket of bones, he carefully picked the plants the skunk had said to select. He pounded the plants into a pulp, and put the pulp into the troll's water pot.

That night David served Plumblump a big bowl of water. The troll bolted down the water in the big bowl and belched. Then plop, before Plumblump could put himself to bed, he fell asleep on the floor.

David poked his finger into Plumblump's paunch once, twice, three times, but the sleeping troll just snored. David needed to find the key for his collar and proceeded to put his hands into Plumblump's pockets.

A dead toad in one pocket, a mouse trap with mouse in another, a rusty knife. Ah. The key. David clicked the key in the lock and the collar fell off.

He was ready to run away, but took time to think. If he left the troll loose it might keep trying to kidnap him. So David clicked the collar onto the troll's neck. Let him eat mushrooms and roots and worms for a while.

David put the key in his pocket and ran away home. He just had time to dust and sweep before bedding down.

The next morning David's grandma returned in the wagon.

"I hope the Franklin family was hospitable," she said.

David knew she didn't know she'd forgotten to arrange accommodations.

"Yes, grandma, it was great. What would you like to eat?"

That evening, in the quiet after dinner, David could dimly hear the troll hissing from his cave and shaking the beech tree.

"Sssilly ssson, little lad let me loose. I'm sssorry I sssnuck you away."

But David kept the key in his pocket.

His grandma, although confused and forgetful, could hear the troll as well.

"I hear hissing David, what is that noise?"

"Just the wind whining through the beech leaves grandma, and trembling the tree. You should go to sleep."

Plumblump kept hissing and crying and after a week David began to feel sorry for him. One evening, at dusk, he crawled back under the roots of the beech tree. Plumblump was almost skinny from his diet of roots and mushrooms and worms.

"Plumblump, if I release you, will you solemnly swear to never be seen by me or my grandmother again?"

"Yesss, Plumblump ssssol sssswea, oh that's ssso hard to sssay. I give you my oath.

"Will you swear by Lardilummox?"

"Yesss, even that."

David paused. And will you also swear by Lardilummox to never eat skunk again?

"But ssskunks are ssso sssuculent!"

"Never mind. Will you swear?"

"Yesss, Plumblump ssswears.

And so David released the troll and he and his grandma went back to living just as they had before. David never saw the troll or the skunks again, but every Friday evening he would put two hen's eggs at the base of the beech, and every Saturday morning there would just be egg shells and the faint, faint odor of skunk.

52.
The Dun Horse
Edward Ahern

Below is a substantially rewritten version of "The Dun Horse." This tale was collected on the Pawnee reservation by George Bird Grinnel and published in 1889 in his book titled "Pawnee Hero stories and Folk Tales."

An Indian named Eagle Chief (warrior name White Eagle) on learning of Grinnel's mission said:

"It is good and it is time. Already the old things are being lost, and those who knew the secrets are many of them dead. If we had known how to write we would have put these things down and they would not have been forgotten. But we could not write and these stories were handed down from one to another. The old men told their grandchildren and so the secrets and the stories and the doings of long ago have been handed down. It may be that they have changed as they passed from father to son, and it is well that they should be put down so that our children, when they are like the white people, can know what were their fathers' ways."

This is my homage to "The Dun Horse." I hope you like it too.

****

Long ago in the Pawnee tribe there lived an old woman and her grandson, a boy of sixteen. These two had no living relatives in the tribe and were very poor. The rest of the tribe despised them for having nothing, not even family.

The old woman and the boy always stayed behind when the tribe moved to new hunting grounds so they could search through the trash of the abandoned camp for things the other Pawnees had thrown away—shreds of buffalo robes, worn-out moccasins with holes in them and chunks of old bone and gristle.

One day as the old woman and her grandson followed behind on the trail of their tribe, they walked up to an old, bony dun horse which had been left to die by another band of Indians.

The dun horse swayed, worn out, thin, blind in one eye, with a sore back and swollen foreleg. The horse was in such poor condition that none of the Indians had been willing to drive it along with them on the trail.

But the old woman and the boy were not so fussy. They were used to having almost nothing. "Grandmother," said the boy, "let's put a rope on this old horse and have him carry our pack."

And the old woman tied their small pack on the sore backed horse. They started to drive the horse along with them, but he limped badly and could only stumble along slowly.

Their Pawnee tribe had moved along the North Platte river until they came to a place now called Court House Rock. A week after they had pitched their camp the old woman and the boy slowly walked in with the dun horse.

Two days later some young braves who had been sent out to scout for buffalo came riding quickly back into the camp. They had found a large herd of buffalo nearby, and among the buffalos was a spotted calf, a rare, rare thing.

A robe made from a spotted calf is ti-war'-uka-ti, big medicine. When the head chief of the Pawnee tribe heard of the calf he ordered his crier to go through the camp and call out that the man who killed the spotted calf should have the chief's daughter for a wife.

The other chiefs agreed to a race to the buffalo herd from the village, so that the man with the fastest horse would be most likely to kill the calf and win the daughter.

The young braves picked out their fastest horses and got ready for the hunt, even the poor boy on his dun horse. The rich young braves sat on their quick horses and laughed at the poor boy on his sway backed dun horse. "See, this is the horse that will catch up to the spotted calf!"

The poor boy was ashamed and rode slowly away to one side of the crowd of horsemen so he would not hear the cruel things the braves said about him.

After they had ridden away the dun horse stopped suddenly, turned his head around and spoke to the boy. "Take me down to the creek and plaster me all over with mud. Cover my face and neck, and body and legs."

The boy was startled when he heard the horse speak, but he did as he was asked. After the boy had slapped mud all over the horse's body the dun said, "mount me now, but do not ride back to the warriors who laugh at you. Stay here until they begin their charge to the feeding grounds."

Soon all the fine horses were drawn up in a line, prancing. At last the old crier yelled "Loo-ah" – Go!

The Pawnee warriors leaned forward, yelled and galloped off. Suddenly, far to the right, the dun horse was seen. He did not seem to gallop, but to sail through the tall grasses. The dun horse soon passed the other horses and rode into the buffalo herd. The horse charged past many buffalo and rode up to the spotted calf. The poor boy shot his arrow, U-ra-rish! The arrow flew hard and straight and the spotted calf fell.

The boy drew another arrow, U-ra-rish! and killed a fat cow that was running by. Then he jumped off the dun horse and began to skin the spotted calf before any of the other warriors could ride up.

When the other warriors rode up and saw the old dun horse, how changed it was. It pranced all about the dead calf and would barely stand still. Its back was clean and shiny, its legs were strong and both eyes were clear and bright.

After skinning the spotted calf and the cow the boy loaded the meat and cow robe on the dun horse and lashed the spotted robe on top. Even under the heavy load of meat and hides the dun horse pranced and was skittish.

As the boy was leading the horse back to camp a rich young chief rode up to him and offered the boy twelve good horses for the spotted robe, for the young chief wanted to marry the head chief's beautiful daughter. But the boy just laughed at the chief and would not sell the robe.

Other warriors had ridden back to camp first. One rode up to the old woman and said," Your grandson has killed the spotted calf!"

The old woman got angry. "Why do you tell me this? You should be ashamed to make fun of my grandson because he is poor."

"What I tell you is true," said the warrior and rode off.

A little later another brave rode up to the old woman, "Your grandson has killed the spoted calf." The old woman tried not to cry. She felt bad that everyone was making fun of her grandson.

Soon the boy walked into camp leading the dun horse up to his grandmother's lodge. It was a little lodge, just enough for two people, made of old pieces of skin the grandmother had found, tied together with strings of rawhide and sinew. It was the worst lodge in the camp.

The boy stopped at the lodge and when the grandmother saw the dun horse loaded with meat and robes she could not speak for shock.

"Here," the boy said, "I have brought you plenty of meat to eat, and here is a cow robe that you can have for yourself. Haul the meat from the horse."

And the old woman laughed, for her heart was glad. But when she tried to pull the meat from the dun horse's back the horse jumped and bucked as if wild. The woman could not believe it was the same horse. Finally the boy had to unload the horse himself, although it was not his work, for it would not allow the woman to come near.

That night when the boy walked out of the lodge to check on the dun horse, the horse spoke to him again. "Wat-ti-nes Chah-ra-rat wa-ta. Tomorrow Sioux come, a large war party. They will attack the camp, and there will be a great fight. When the Sioux are lined up for battle, jump on me and ride into the middle of them. Ride to the head chief, their greatest warrior, count coup on him, kill him, and ride back. Do this four times, count coup on three more of the bravest Sioux and kill them, but do not ride out a fifth time. If you return a fifth time you will either die or you will lose me."

The boy promised. The next day, as the horse had said, the Sioux came to the camp and formed a line of battle. The boy jumped on the dun horse and charged into them.

When the Sioux saw that the boy was trying to strike their chief they shot arrows so thickly the sky was black, but none touched him. And the boy counted coup on the chief, killed him, and rode back. Four times the boy did this, as the horse had told him.

But the Sioux and the Pawnee kept fighting and the boy stood back next to the dun horse watching the battle. At last he felt ashamed that he was not in the battle and thought, "I have been in battle four times and have beaten four Sioux. I am not hurt anywhere; why can I not go in again?"

The boy jumped on the dun horse and rode back into the battle. As soon as he rode in a Sioux chief shot an arrow that struck the dun horse behind the forelegs, piercing him through. The dun horse fell down dead, but the boy got up and fought his way back through the Sioux to the Pawnees.

After the dun horse had dropped the Sioux said among themselves, "This horse was like a man. He was brave. He was not like a horse." So they did as they would do to a brave man, and cut the horse into pieces with their knives and hatchets.

The Pawnee and the Sioux fought all day long, but toward nightfall the Sioux warriors broke and fled.

That night after the battle the boy left the village to mourn for his horse. He went to where his horse lay, gathered the pieces and put them together in a pile. Then the boy went to the top of a nearby hill, pulled his spotted calf robe over his head and began to mourn for his horse.

As he crouched there a great wind storm roared over him in rushing waves, and after the wind came rain. The boy looked down at what was left of his horse, but could barely see it through the rain. Then the rain passed.

Then came another roaring wind and, after it, again rain. The boy looked down at the pile and through the rain it looked like a horse lying down, but he could barely see through the driving water.

A third storm came, like the others, and when he looked down at the horse he thought he could see the tail move and the horse's head lift from the ground. The boy was afraid, and thought about running away, but stayed to mourn his horse.

A fourth storm came and as the rain pounded down the dun horse raised up on its forelegs, looked around, and stood up.

Although filled with fear the boy left the hilltop and walked down to the horse. The dun horse said," You have seen how it has been this day; and from this you may know how it will be after. Ti-ra-wa has been good and let me come back to you. After this, do what I tell you, not any more, not any less."

And the horse said, "Now lead me away from the camp until we are behind that big hill. Leave me there tonight and in the morning come for me."

The boy did as he was told, and when he came back in the morning he saw the dun horse with a fine white gelding, handsomer than any other horse in the tribe.

For ten nights the boy did this and each morning he found another horse, a black gelding, a bay, a roam, a blue spotted; all finer than any horses the Pawnees had ever before had in their tribe.

Now the boy was rich, and he married the beautiful daughter of the head chief. In time the boy was made head chief. He always took good care of his old grandmother, and kept her in his own lodge until she died. He had many children, and one day, when his oldest son died, he wrapped him in the spotted calf robe,

The dun horse was never ridden except at a feast or a dance, and was led around wherever the chief went. The horse lived in the Pawnee camps for many years and became very old. And at last he died.

54.
The Emergent Poet at Fifty
Michael D. Jones

Some things I never tire of
Like reflections of the moon
(The big early moon seen through trees)
On water or any large window.
Apple fritters and cigars for breakfast
And a few hours or eighteen
Dew wetted holes to burn at play.
Good poetry-
Not great, just well-crafted and smacking
Of truth.
Acres of husky stalks of corn, chest-high
In windswept fields where clouds
Of birds dive and whirl, then settle
Beneath the golden waves.
Matinee Tigers' baseball in May
Or late September, but not midsummer.
Frothy whitecaps as the day heats
And gusts relentlessly from the west
Over the big lake.
Barbeque anything
Especially grilled salmon and asparagus
With Cesar salad and Pinot Noir.
Bats at dusk feeding on invisibly small
And illusive mosquitoes, swollen
From their last meal.
Nearly uncontrollable bonfires
Surrounded by
Marshmallows ready to also burst.
Friends that harmlessly flirt

And are unabashedly good at it.
Wink, wink.
Waking up pre-dawn with the dull ache
Of yesterday's landscape labors
And needing to go, then climbing back
Into the warm bed, drowsy
Vaguely satisfied, and stiff.
These days and nights, and things
That play with light.
Is this so wrong to admit?   *Wink.*

54.
The Filigreed Lamp
Edward Ahern

Once, not so long ago, a young girl named Kestrel lived on a farm. Kestrel's hair was the same gold-brown color as her namesake hawk, and she darted about with the agility of a kestrel in flight.

One day a construction company came to the farm and began to dig a long trench for a gas pipeline. The trench cut right through an overgrown, gnarly gully, good for nothing and left alone by everyone.

After they had laid the pipe and filled in the hole, Kestrel walked down the packed earth as if it were a path made just for her. When she reached the gully she looked down from her path and saw that the diggers had sheared off part of the gully's bank, exposing a little brick wall where none should be. No one had ever used the gully for anything.

Kestrel slid down the embankment to the bricks. She saw that the bricks were laid to seal an opening into the hillside. The bricks were oddly shaped and discolored with age. The mortar between the bricks was half crumbled away. Kestrel kicked at the bricks and they broke loose, falling back into the opening.

A peculiar smell blew out of the little cave, like cooking oil and incense. Kestrel wasn't afraid of mice or spiders, and pushed enough of the bricks aside so she could crawl in. The dirt ceiling brushed against her hair as she crawled. There was nothing there. Well, almost nothing. On a flat rock, in the middle of the little cave, all by itself, was an odd looking pitcher, or gravy boat, or maybe an oil can. It was covered with dust, and the dust had congealed into a layer of dirt.

When Kestrel picked up the pitcher she almost dropped it again. It was really heavy, as if it were solid stone. She picked at the dirt, flaking it off. Underneath were flashes of silver and gold. Kestrel had nothing to use to wipe off the pitcher. She looked down at her pants, already covered in brick dust and dirt. They have to be washed anyway, she thought, and began rubbing the jug on the thighs of her Jeans.

"I think you've rubbed me out."

The voice made Kestrel drop the pitcher. She would have run, but she would have had to crabble around on her knees before she could face the entry.

"Clumsy, I see. Try not to drop that again. It's unsettling."

It was a woman's voice, liquid and soft.

"Where—where are you?" Kestrel quavered.

"Ah yes, a little light on the situation." The words were chewy.

Light swelled up from the thing on the floor, not day light, but the yellow flicker that an oil lamp makes. Kestrel stared at the most peculiarly dressed young woman she had ever seen. Her dark hair was wrapped in braids around the top of her head like a turban. Her slippers were pointed and looked like lake blue silk. She wore red pants and jacket embroidered in gold. She had the complexion of a porcelain doll, with the same pouting lips.

"What? How? Who?" Kestrel muttered.

"Don't babble, dear, it's not becoming. It's my bad luck that you found the lamp and summoned me. All right, let's get started."

"I don't understand."

The woman sighed. "Are you still reading fairy tales?"

"Sometimes."

"What happens when you rub a certain lamp?"

"Oh. You're a Genii—I get wishes! But you're a woman?"

"Don't call me Genii. I am a Jinn. Jeanie is what you call a waitress in a diner. I appear to you as a woman because it's easier for you to grasp. Usually I get a chest thumping man, and he sees me as bigger and meaner than he is."

Kestrel had been poised to jump backward out of the cave. But this was too interesting. She settled back on her haunches.

"Do I get three wishes?"

"Your requests are unlimited, but there are rules."

"How can there be rules on wishes? I can wish for whatever I like."

"No, you squiggly little eel, you can't. What's your name?"

"Kestrel."

"Listen to the rules, Kestrel." The Jinn waved its arms jointlessly, as if they were made of smoke.

"You cannot ask for what must be freely given—love and friendship, for example.

"You cannot change an inner state—happiness, sadness, pride, greed—in yourself or others.

"You cannot alter the inevitable—such as aging and dying."

Kestrel thought for a moment. "That still leaves lots of things I can ask for."

"Ah, yes, but in addition to the rules there is a caution. The more selfish your request the more likely your wish is to betray you—like lighting a forest fire with the wind howling in your face. Even a good hearted request may have painful consequences."

"But I can keep making wishes until good things happen."

"I can almost hear your monkey mind whirring. Know that none of the men who have disturbed my freedom have ever asked for more than three wishes."

Kestrel was puzzled. "Wait, ah, what should I call you?"

"Alephriel."

"Alephriel, you said freedom. Weren't you trapped inside the lamp until I rubbed it? Aren't you grateful to me to be out?"

"No, sparrow hawk, your fable tellers have gotten it wrong for four millennia. I'm free when I'm not groveling in a cave granting wishes. When you disturbed me I was in the middle of my second century inside a volcano, flowing with swirls of magma struggling to be stone."

"Wow. Do I have to ask for something now?'

"No, the only limit is your lifetime. Take the lamp with you until you know what you want. No one can take it from you until you release me. And you should clean it. It's disgusting looking. Goodbye."

The lamp light went out. Alephriel was gone. Kestrel picked up the lamp and crawled on her elbows and knees back out of the cave. She would have run home, but the lamp was too heavy. Kestrel walked behind their house and used the garden hose to wash off the lamp. The lamp was covered with silver and gold filigree, with symbols etched on its back.

Kestrel put the lamp in the bottom drawer of her bureau, under her t-shirts, and began to think. That night, after supper but before she went to sleep, Kestrel took out the lamp and rubbed it.

"Not even one day and you're already making a wish?"

Alephriel was sitting on Kestrel's bed. She wore a cloak of ink black silk and under it an apple red dress. Her short hair was red and tightly curled. But the face was the same, smooth and serene, with pouty lips.

"Don't you ever dress the same?"

"No, little daughter, when I'm dragged out I like to dress up."

"I know what I want."

"Do you now? No one else ever really did. What is it?"

"Something small, something kind, something not for me. My father broke his big toe when he was a boy, and he's always walked with a little limp because it hurts. Fix his toe, please."

"So you have spoken, so it shall be."

That next morning Kerstrel saw her father pacing back and forth in the upstairs corridor, still in his pajamas.

"What's wrong dad?"

"It's what's right that has me worried, Kes. My toe doesn't hurt anymore. I'm wondering if I have nerve damage or if it's infected."

Kestrel almost giggled. "Gee, dad, maybe you should just be happy that it doesn't hurt."

The doctor could find nothing wrong, and Kestrel's father was so happy that he thought about taking dancing lessons. And then, while walking down the stairs he forgot that his toe was better, stepped like he had a limp, lost his balance, and fell all the way down, breaking his leg.

Kestrel's father came back from the hospital with his leg in a cast. She pulled the lamp out of the bottom drawer and rubbed it so hard her hand hurt.

"Don't wear off the filigree," Alephriel said.

Kestrel was mad. "That's not fair! My dad shouldn't have to suffer because his toe got better!"

Alephriel was twirling around while Kestrel spoke. Her hair was blonde and bouffant, and she wore a green mini skirt with spangled leggings under a pink sweatshirt that said, "EAT GREASE." But her lips were still pouty.

"Kestrel, my child, I warned you about unintended consequences. Everything we do has an effect. But don't worry. Your father's leg will heal, and he'll still take those dancing lessons."

Kestrel waited two more weeks before she summoned Alephriel again. Alephriel was dressed all in black leather, boots up through pants and jacket and black leather cap. Her hair was shaved off, but she had kept her pearly complexion and pouty expression.

"Okay Alephriel, I've got it now. My best friend is Marissa. Her family is really poor, so poor that Marissa has no clothes for school and never has any money for lunch. I wish for her family to become rich, so Marissa can have everything she wants."

Alephriel looked sad. "That's really what you want?"

"Yes, absolutely."

"So you have spoken, so it shall be."

Marissa's family was contacted the next day by a private investigator. An uncle no one had ever heard of had died and left them a big inheritance, Marissa was given clothes, and toys, and jewelry. She was taken from the public school where she and Kestrel went, and placed in a private school. She made new friends, and forgot about the old ones.

Kestrel telephoned Marissa several times, but they never met, and Marissa finally told Kestrel that her new friends and tutors and special lessons left her no time at all for Kestrel. Kestrel cried a little, and waited a week, and rubbed the lamp again.

Alephriel wore a flouncy, white bridal dress, with white satin slippers and a white veil on top of long auburn hair "This is truly uncomfortable. It's no wonder you people only wear it once."

Kestrel started crying again. "How could I make such a mistake, Alephriel?"

"It's not your fault, child. Some people change with their circumstances But I strongly suspect that by the time you both go to college you'll be friends again."

"How can you be sure?"

"Her family will have spent all the money. Did you summon me to make a wish?"

"Not a wish, Alephriel. I'm not doing too well with those. But I wanted to ask you about where you go when you're inside the lamp. You mentioned a volcano?"

"Ah child, it's too bad you can't survive these things or I'd show you. Yes, the last time was a volcano, a wonderful, rich mineral soup, so hot things lost their identity, and changed and reformed and changed again. The best hot, soaking bath you ever took would be a tiny taste of where I was.

"And before that, for two of your lifetimes, I swam in a huge lake under a glacier at the South Pole, an ice shell surrounding a yolk of water older than mankind, with only the faintest memories of the living things that once swam in it.

"And before that for almost two hundred tree rings I rose and fell with the sap of a huge oak that druids worshipped, sharing in the growth and fall of leaves and acorns. So, yes, when I'm in the lamp I'm truly free."

Kestrel made no more wishes, but she thought and thought about what Alephriel had told her. After two long months she rubbed the lamp again.

Alephriel bounced off the bed, clad in bright purple spandex, her white hair sprawling from her head like a shaving brush.. "This material should be banned because of body distortion. All my soft parts are squished and my bony bits protrude. Really!"

"Alephriel, I've been thinking."

"A dangerous pursuit for the best of humans."

"I want to make another wish."

"That's a pity. What is your wish?"

Kestrel smiled at Alephriel. "I know that you really love your freedom. But I think you complain a little too much about having to associate with humans. You do enjoy being with us for at least a little while. What you don't like is being yanked around by us willy-nilly. So, what I wish, what I want for you, is that you alone control when you appear to us. You're four thousand years old, you should be adult enough to handle it."

Alephriel's pouty lips broke into a smile. "So you have spoken, so it shall be. I'm actually closer to seven thousand years old. How did you know that once I was free, I wouldn't do you and others harm?"

"Because you don't interfere. You take part, but you don't disrupt things."

Alephriel shimmered, her clothing and hair molting several times in a second. "Free at last. Kestrel, please keep the lamp for me."

"I will. It's just a lamp now, but it's pretty. I can't demand any more wishes, but could you please stop by every once in a while and tell me about your trips?"

"My next trip, Kestrel, will last longer than your lifetime, but I promise that before I leave, I'll come back and tell you about other wishes and other trips."

55.
The Haunting
Shannon Waite

I'm lying on my side, facing the window to the left of me, where I watch the street lamps highlight the snowflakes that are collecting on the sill. The snowflakes all look identical, but I know better than that. I know that they're unique. I know that they are made of intricate shapes. I know that they are all delicate. I know that I could probably spend more time thinking about them, but you...

All that I can think about now is you.

It's like you are trapped inside of my skeleton, invading the caverns that house my soul, and you can't seem to find a way to escape, so you are screaming at me. You're clawing at my muscle and flesh, scratching through my oily, bitter pores, and I cry because I can't escape you. You are all that I think about anymore. You are all that I want anymore and is it sad to say that I find comfort in the fact that I can't get away? I quickly forget about the cold winter days and I delve into all of these thoughts of you.

Your haunting, porcelain face—oh, the edges are soft and chiseled like the perfect outline of a faint ghost. Your butterfly-kiss eyelashes. They wiggle at me as I stare. They wave and blow signs of affection towards the wind, but I want them. I want them to blow signs of affection towards me. Your lips look like petals, out-turned and pouty, against your fragile snow-blanket skin... and they look so beautiful; you look so beautiful, and you haunt me next to another, growing monster inside of my stomach, but I give in because he is a part of you and that is really all that I want.

This monster kind of fascinates me; he creates this sense of eeriness that I can't run from. I feel the tips of his pseudo claws punch holes into my stomach lining as he grips onto the walls of my insides and climbs up my throat. His feet are kicking my esophagus and I can't help but gag. It's terrible, all of this, but all of this pain that I endure is for you. It's so that maybe, for one more night, I will be able to see your face in my dreams as you haunt them. Your innocence and sincerity. Your beauty. I can't handle not having you anymore. I just can't do it.

Every action that I take is in light of you. I can't help but stop and think about what you would do if you were in this situation, or how you might let it play out. My mind flickers between this imaginary person that I've created in absence of you, and the results leave shadows that quickly fade inside of my mind. I don't like when they fade... It hurts.

I'm an average guy—or at least I used to be. There wasn't anything too exciting, but then again, every now and then something would happen that would keep me on my toes. I ate toast for breakfast, downed a few cups of coffee, inhaled a few packs of cigarettes, politely kissed my wife on her cheek, sat at my desk and stared at some papers, came home, and went to bed. Yes, that was my life. Now, however, my life has been consumed by you. I am no longer a person, but rather, a product. My shelf life is coming to an end and I'll soon be useless to the rest of society, but you, my dear, are what I thrive for. Although my outside is just a shell, my insides blossom for you.

I long for your touch and your laugh. For the noises that you make when you scream and cry. As you whimper and distort your pretty little face. For your presence. I long for it all, and all of these thoughts of you are what have molded me into such a worthless guy.

Sometimes, I stare at myself in the mirror and wonder what happened to me. My eyes are sunken and shifty. I rub my palm against the "shadow" that's appearing on my face and I feel scrapes. I should probably fix that but I don't. I notice the weight that is creeping onto my body but I don't care. You don't care, so I don't.

Why should I have my own thoughts when I can borrow yours? There's something more poetic about them, I guess.

They're with me at all times anyways and no one hears me, no one knows, but they are.

After all, me and you? I keep us a secret. Our relationship. Our eternal love that I grasp onto so tightly. My knuckles burn and transform into a buttermilk white shade with wrinkled skin, but still I hold on. My unkempt nails dig underneath my flesh and draw drops of blood to the surface that lick the fresh air that they've just now met. My muscles twist and break down just to bring themselves back up. Yes, I hold on so tightly, but really, just for that last taste of our love—it's worth it, my darling.

Yes. You're worth it.

It's been years since I've pressed my lips unto my wife's. Since I've ran my strong hands against her soft body. Since I've interwoven my fingers into the twisted locks of her hair. Since I've looked in her eyes and have actually seen her. It's been years, and do you know why?

It's because of you.

Now, Miss Michigan is no longer a sufficient resource for me even. And as for my wife, it's not like I didn't try, because I did. But every time that I placed a cupped palm over her chest, or started running my tongue down her salty body, I thought of you, damnit. That's all that I thought about. So now, the relationship that she and I have is comparative to an empty, stone basement. On the rare occasions that we both sit across from each other at our breakfast table, and the rare moments that we both look up from our separate papers, and the rare instances that our eyes both meet, I see nothing. I see emptiness. I see loss.

I mean, maybe I'm wrong. Sometimes a hint of longing and confusion surfaces, but just slightly, until her irises re-submerge and suppress the tattle that her heart is confessing. It hurts, because I remember the time that I was once in love with her. The time when walking through the door wasn't a chore or a routine, but rather an adventure. The time when I looked at her and smiled because she was everything in my world. She represented my hopes and dreams; the better side of me. But again, that was years ago, and now we're lucky if neither of us says a word and if we both continue on with our day.

I bring home money for our food. I put my clothes in the corner of our room and a few days later, she returns them to the same corner in neat, little, clean piles.

We coexist on the most inhumane level of existence and just barely pass by each other.

But this... this is because of you. My nerve endings have electrified themselves. They no longer have feeling. The only feeling that I now know is the one that you have produced with this monster that I relentlessly take care of, because that's what I do. Nothing says that I am required to nurture him, but I do. He feeds off of the thoughts that I have, and as a result, this artificial monster doesn't have anywhere else to burrow but my stomach.

And I'd cry. Oh, I would cry if I could, but I can't. I'm void of almost any emotion now. I feel like I've transformed into an exoskeleton. A shell that wanders Earth. Most of the time, I feel like I simply exist just to take up space.

This life is such a hassle at points, but I continue on with the hopes of crossing your path again. The hopes of touching your sweet skin again haunt my thoughts. I imagine your wind bitten cheeks caressing mine. It really is just a haunting memory that I think I've probably made up, but it's all that's left of me, really.

As my body rots incessantly, and my bones decompose and decay underneath the soil that starts to encase my body, you are all that I will have left. Your skin lays with mine. Your eyes are reflected in mine. My heart will have stopped beating and maggots will crawl in the holes and make it their home, but that's fine. I guess that the way that I look at it is just this way: at least my body will be of use to something since it was never any use to me. I guess I see it as my way of giving back.

Goodness, the future aside, Love, you are my breaths. In this moment, you are my breaths and you are the steps that I take. You are my history. My past, my present, and my future. You are everything that I want but can't have. Baby, I think that I'm obsessed. I think that I have a problem that I don't know how to solve. I think that, maybe, I'm in love with you.

Tonight, I lay down in bed on my side. The side that's closest to the window, farthest from the lamp. She lies on her side, the one with the lamp and the one without the window. We have a foot between us. An empty, cavernous foot. It looms there, almost taunting us, and neither one of us crosses it. Ever. Tonight, I want to try. Tonight, well, tonight is one of the nights that I feel brave, so I roll. I cautiously turn over, not facing the window with my back to her as usual. I'm now facing her, instead, with my slow breaths creeping down her spine and I know that she's confused. I know that she doesn't understand it but it's alright. I don't think that I understand either.

I stare at her back for a while. I study its contours and its shape. I study the lighting and the shadows that it makes and I study her movement. There's none and it's almost as if she isn't even alive.

I guess I understand. I'm not really alive anymore either. I wonder sometimes if living is contagious or if it is something that we just do. Can we lose the ability to do it? ...I think that we can.

I muster up my courage and with the feeling of all of the weight of an anchor stitched below my skin it takes so much effort to move my arm. I reach over and with the very tips of my fingers, I touch her body and she's stiff as a stone. She's cold, and clammy, and very much a corpse. Her hair is no longer in delicate locks, but rather it's entangled, wiry, and in clumps.

She's awake. I know it. She's just not responding.

Well, I've tried. I pull my hand back and return to the indicated position that I sleep in. She is facing the lamp and I am facing the window. Our backs are facing each other's and we have a very empty foot between us.

So now, I return to thinking of you.

I am the corpse of a father and I think that I'm in love with my unborn daughter.

She has destroyed me and my wife and I've nowhere else to turn but to the window on my left.

56.
The Hush
Diana Kathryn Plopa

When you touched me with your tenderness
Behind my eyes grew a well of tears
For the magnificence of your power
Opened treasures not revealed in all my years

The reflection of your spirit
Radiated from just behind your eyes
The gentleness of your sincerity
Brought to me a multitude of starlit skies

When you caressed my soul with a whisper
Delving deep into the person I am
My entire body trembled with undeniable rapture
As your encouragement softly took command

Then you wrapped me warmly in a blanket
Quiet music and a silken touch
Your arms enveloped me as we drifted to sleep
Together we embraced the wonder found in The Hush

57.
The Naturalist in the Woods
John Grey

It makes no sense to him
why the weekend hunter
has to kill an innocent fellow creature.
He says he'd sooner see a man die than a black bear.

The creature's been shot
who knows how many miles back,
has lugged its wounded body over a rocky hill
and down into a ravine.
But now all that's left to that poor blood-soaked beast
is the misery of dying,
a leg too shattered to ever heal,
a head cocked to one side,
pain grasping even tighter
with each startled roar.

A man he says
can regret his sins
at the end
or gather his loved ones
or relive his life
at a pace commensurate
with how long he's got,
and he can leave out the bad
while he's doing it.

But what's the bear to do
when the sense of himself starts fading,
and he's left with a cold dark nothingness.
the greatest bear trap of all.

Yes, he says sadly,
it was a man who did this to the poor creature,
a man he'd rather see die in its place.

Then he adds that a bear is wild
because that's its nature.
And a man is wild
because a bear is wild.

58.
The Personal Ad
Shannon Waite

"To live is the rarest thing in the world; most people just exist."

Objectified. Coerced. Abandoned.

My breath felt soft as I felt my heartbeats fall in line with the rhythm of the words that I was reading; the letters were scrawled in black permanent marker, with bolded outlines, on the ripped-edge paper. They screamed my name so loudly as I felt myself sink into the shadows of the apartment... and that's just it... I felt it. I felt all of it.

I traced my fingertip against these words that were screaming sentiments at me: awful, disgusting, lousy, sickening, inconvenient, and worthless. They echoed so loudly that the traffic outside was nothing but a quiet hum. Instead, I listened to these words on repeat as they started to take the shape of my skin, and bones, and body. I had never seemed to look so articulate before.

It's amazing how inked symbols translate to more than just colors or images, but rather, they can ignite emotion and drag out memories too. I let my eyes wander around the letters on the pages and I let my mind dwell on their meaning and I felt my heart breaking as I realized that you really meant them.

Sometimes, my skin wants to crawl far, far away from my body, and sometimes, I wish I could just push it off of my bones. I wish I could rip the embedded bickering out of my ear lobes and I could just find a hole in someone's heart to climb inside and hide in, but then I realize... I've actually been in a hole all along.

As I curled my legs into a comfortable, Indian-style sitting position, I brushed messes of hair out of my face. I let the written words on the journal pages sitting on the floor haunt me as I began to realize that I didn't love you anymore. That's right—I didn't love you anymore. But how could I? You never loved me. I looked at the words that you called me; the words that you claimed I was: these words, written across the scattered pages on the floor—and then I realized—I felt them, too, more than I even saw them.

Slowly, I bit my lip, teeth slicing flesh and blood rushing to the surface, because blood tasted better than sweat. You see, sweat meant work, and work was something that I wouldn't do. I promised myself that I wouldn't. No, not for you. Not anymore, at least.

I started to realize that this was it: this was going to be the last night that I would hold onto anything in regards to you. Instead, I was going to let it all go because that meant that I was letting go of the weight.

I was not about to face the monster that I didn't love though, so I hoped that you would figure it out on your own; my departure was out of pure entropy because no longer would I remain inside of a hole that was broken; after all, something that is broken cannot support a person.

I picked myself up, and in the confines of the shaded black room that I was in, I walked towards the large mirror that was hanging on the wall. Now looking at the one I hated so much, I gazed at the silhouetted reflection lingering in it and realized that the diluted image reflected not just my face, but my life too, and I couldn't do it anymore.

I fell out of love.

I fell out of love with the one person who I had to live with, and that was the worst love that I could lose. I didn't want to be surrounded by her anymore, or the words that she continued to identify me with, so I began to craft the new personal ad that I wanted others to read; I desperately wanted someone else, someone whose hole was big enough and strong enough for me to climb inside.

I picked apart a set of new words; words that meant something more; words that might help me find this new love... and with the drag of a small blade down my wrists, and stomach, and thighs, I scribbled the following as one, permanent note:

I am accepting applications for love. Must live in the area. Must hear soft cries. Must view days as significant—and not the tragedies that occur during them as so.

Please include your: Hopes. Dreams and Favorite word.

Please answer the following questions:
I.   When is it convenient for you to love me?
II.   Can you handle passion and motivation?
III. Why? Why do you want to love me?

And with one final slit, I confirmed that blood did taste better than sweat, and that I kept the promise I had made to myself long ago: I would not let you control my life.

I knew that no one would ever answer this ad. I knew that this ad was not actually for anyone else.

So, slowly, I again felt my breath and with one last noiseless heave I embraced a moment of silence, finally.

"To live is the rarest thing in the world; most people just exist."

59.
The Ravishing
Deborah Guzzi

A chill wind nipped coyly at exposed necks,
not yet draped in their tourniquets of wool.
A shawl of white, buries the venous veins of
asphalt as the way fills with horsepower.
Goblets of slush like spittle fall with a splat,
upon the virginal snowfields.
> The rape of winter begins.

Rutting like rabid beasts in heat, the horde
splays the main roadways reveling in power,
creating blowbys—cumulous clouds rise
from mouths of chrome.
> The rape of winter begins.

Winter like the Sabine Women, weaponless,
pummels each vehicle with spears of ice.
Small fists of power fall in weights of white.
> Winter defends herself.

The day's surge brings forth an endless advance:
trampling her breasts, ravaging hollows and
deltas, shredding the veil of purity that
the Goddess Angerona brings. Anguish and
debris lay mud covered as the beauty of
> Winter falls to the metal of man.

The Mother curls inward, her breath freezes
ground down, screeching, shrieking,
She succumbs in ashes of her finery;
she lays vanquished.

60.
The Thinning of the Veil
Deborah Guzzi

The crystal ball snow pierces the biting autumn wind;
parting the dancing, curled, brown, leaves, as they
leap across the lurid landscape. Jack-o-lanterns and
ruby red mums shivered.

Scarecrows on their crossed pickets, lean precariously
against bales of salt marsh hay which wafts in the gale.
Remnants of summer and autumn's lingering greenery,
beat back the black clouds, blotting the light of noon.
Shards of light prick the haze, adding a dreamlike effect.
Day, night, the world awaited Samhain's Eve.

Snow falls frantically from the firmament fighting to
coat the last of the pink cone flowers, and the world
is full of the scent of cider and cinnamon.

61.
The User Used
Diana Kathryn Plopa

Once in quiet solitude
I walked a distant shore
I watched the waves roll in
And subside as in ancient lore
The wonder and the beauty
Took me by surprise
The perfection in its simplicity
The crest of a moonlit tide
Now I walk in a solitude
Interrupted by deafening noise
Screams of fear interjected
With cries of breaking toys
All around me dwells a pressure
Simple existence—a struggle—a fight
I scream as protecting darkness
Gives birth to horror with awakening light
Silently I sit here screaming
With these thoughts that I whore
I yearn for that quiet solitude
For calm to return once more

62.
The Year Without a Summer
Two
Mark Hudson

Source: The Lost German Slave Girl

A different story from the volcanic Tambora,
a shoemaker named Daniel from the lower Rhine.
He got in a ship with his wife Dorothea,
to go to America where everyone dines.
More immigrant families began to decide,
to go on the ships to leave everything behind.
So many had wanted to get on the ride,
they headed for the ship with no chance to rewind.
Amsterdam refugees couldn't survive,
they paid the captain to take them away.
With consumers that signed with promises to abide,
headed for New Orleans throws her waterway,
they all ate peas and bacon and rice.
Daniel's youngest child instantly died,
the kids comforted elders who needed advice.
Most of the passengers died on the ship,
but some made it safely to New Orleans.
they were grateful to get to be done with the trip,
observing sugarcane fields as their scenes.
Ships took people off to escape,
to a land of wine, abundance of grapes.
Did they experience The Grapes of Wrath?
We don't even have any photographs.
We can only imagine that times were hard,
you couldn't buy freedom with a credit card.
But the people preferred the life that was new,
the year without summer brought the surviving few.

63.
Theological Reflection on
The Book Thief
Carmanie Bhatti

Her life when I look
Back, to where she lost her loved
Ones, and now this day

Her life was not that
Easy, her journey was on
Road; narrow, painful

That an innocent
Girl of seven, was looking
For destiny true

She who secretly
Wrote letter to her mother
Knew her mother not

Then she cried in her
Despair, trial, anguish but,
Did not give up hope

She faced circumstance
That told her who her mother
Was, and who herself

When God-created
Humanity faced fear, gloom,
She spoke narration

She had the faith that
She with her light will brighten,
Give hope with her words

That she could spread light
To friends with words alphabets,
And wipe away fear

Nature became her
Enemy, when her actions
Were louder than words

It felt she was words
That had power, infinite
Life ability

Destruction she saw
Of that love she had loved, and
With love saved a book!

She would not see her
Burning, humiliating
In public, dying!

She wanted to save
Some words to speak, some words to
Teach, to touch the hearts

She brought images
To minds of listeners,
Making others see

She carried the torch,
Careful to use, and not be
Visible in foes

She had that wisdom
To use intelligently,
For she called it "sister"

Those who had nothing
To feed themselves, gave her a
Title of "daughter"

Then the vocation
And superordination
Became part of them!

They laid their lives in
Danger, for a man they owed once,
To return favor

But that was not the
Only cause they had, they were
Neighbors to stranger

A stranger who came
With no proof of who he was,
But a claim, and help

They refused him not,
Stepping into his shoes, being
Good shepherd of sheep

His rivals became
Fierce, his faith, hope, and love, all
Abided in him

And though he had to
Leave his dear ones, God took care
Of his faith, food, life

So the Lord was his
Shepherd, visiting him in
Hunger, thirst, danger

He who hid himself
Away from his enemies,
Thanked God in open!

His departure was
To the valleys of death, gloom,
To keep others safe!

His beloved though
Left alone in the world was
Under God's eye still

Still she survived, still
Her words were about hope, faith,
And love, which God blessed

Weeping, molesting
Took its part, but new morning,
Rejoicing was there now!

She was a shrub once,
Being trampled on the roadway,
At last she had grown

Her tears were precious
Seen by God, her innocent
Bruise was to give life

The light had now shined
In darkness, and so darkness
Could not overcome!

She grew at full length
Deserved honor of being
A fruit tree with "fruit"

And so this honor
Was an honor to her, her
"Faith," "hope," "love," God's grace!

64.
They Don't Make 'em Like They Used To
Mary Ann Back

My parents, Harry and Alice, married in 1946. Someone gave them a General Electric toaster and unwittingly began, what we children later came to call, "The Great Cincinnati Toaster War" – a conflict that turned our 1950's kitchen into a battlefield. Seldom has an appliance fought so hard to hold its ground.   Tenacity is hard to come by in a toaster.

This chrome-plated warrior survived four moves, a lightning strike, and three little hellions who courted disaster on a daily basis. The toaster was a wily opponent. It used its anaconda-like cord to ensnare us as we passed by the kitchen table, causing both child and toaster to take spectacular spills. Its shiny exterior reflected many a monkey face. With its curious bowed edges, the toaster resembled an Airstream camper. It would be fun to know how many slices of bread it toasted over the years.

My father, a man who could fix anything, was obsessed with this toaster. He quietly accepted upgrades in housing, furniture, and décor over the years but his foot came down on the toaster. Some things were sacred. A man's toaster was his domain.

My mother's goal in life was to replace that toaster, whether through divine intervention, or its having been mysteriously smashed to smithereens, was inconsequential.   Over the years, she softened a bit when it came to my father's attachment to the toaster but she never understood it.

She caught glimpses of victory here and there. The toaster would take a turn for the worse but somehow Dad managed to snatch it from the jaws of death. Sometimes, it wouldn't brown the bread. Dad would tinker with it. Other times, it superheated the bread into carbon. Dad would adjust it. Occasionally, the bread browned but wouldn't eject. Sometimes, bread launched from the toaster like flat, flaming missiles. My brothers and I would yell, "Incoming!" and duck. Dad would fix it. When the cord frayed, he taped it; and when the cord wore completely through, he taped it again. These life sustaining measures continued until one day, after fifty-five years of service, the toaster went up in a blaze of glory. The dutiful toaster departed this world, and with it, a part of my father.

Today's toasters, with their bagel settings, defrosting units, and ridiculously short cords are designed with planned obsolescence. When they break, we throw them away. We buy new. As a society, that's who we've become. We no longer appreciate the fortitude of the brave little toasters that served us with distinction. New is better. Except when it isn't.

Sometimes, that's how we treat the people in our lives. When relationships break, we throw them away. We've lost the capacity to tolerate imperfection in others. We lack the tenacity and forgiveness of those who have gone before us, the Harrys and Alices of the world, who learned the art of compromise and the value of fixing the things that were broken in their lives.

I want to be more like my parents. I want to learn to tolerate people and their curious edges, to rise above the spectacular spills they cause me to take from time to time. Perhaps, when no one is looking, I'll drift back to those simpler days and stare into the side of that toaster. If I'm lucky, I'll rediscover the monkey that used to stare back at me.

65.
Under A Darkening Sky
Terry Sanville

A feather from my right wing flutters downward into the canyon. My mate circles above me. She dives toward the black quill and snatches it in her beak before it can drop into the oaks and sycamores that crowd the creek. Climbing, she flies past me, rolling in the soft afternoon air, croaking with delight, like she did as a young raven before we paired. She's still playful after more than a decade of summers, though her feathers are as ragged as mine.

Our nest is old and used by many others before us. It sits in the crotch of a huge eucalyptus on a hillside overlooking the harbor. Directly below rests an orange-tiled estate where we hunt for bugs under its eaves, drink from the fountain, and bask in the afternoon sun on its roof. As young birds we flew the island's entire length to play with our brethren who nest in the cliffs near the two harbors. But now, we sit on the estate's warm tiles and call to those sailing past. They beckon for us to follow, and when the wind is right, to fly north across the channel to the mainland. But we've flown enough, have claimed our territory, and know how to enjoy our days. The same can't always be said for the humans who live at the estate.

When we first occupied our nest only the man lived in the main house. He stood twice as tall as a fence post with brown hair on top of his pale body. One afternoon he staggered into the flat yard next to the house and slumped into a chair. In one claw, he clutched a bottle half-filled with amber liquid and in the other a glass. His head dripped blood. A woman wearing a dove gray uniform hurried after him. He sat trembling while she cut off his hair and stopped the bleeding. He touched her brown face with his mouth and she pushed him away, but not too hard. They moved inside. We swooped down, snatched up the hair from where it had fallen onto the patio stones, and used it to line the bottom of our nest. It felt soft, perfect for cradling eggs.

It took several moon cycles for the man's hair to grow back, streaked with silver and thinner than before. He spent long days in the yard, staring into the small window of some kind of machine and picking with his claws at its buttoned board with odd markings on it. One day when he'd gone inside, I flew down and pecked at the board. It made weird beeping sounds and the scene in the window changed from a view of our island to strange markings – like those on the sheets of paper that sail through the town when the east wind blows hard. I dipped my beak into his glass of amber liquid. It tasted awful and I choked.

The man must have heard the commotion. He ran into the yard and shooed me away. I ruffled my feathers. My mate and I perched on the rim of our nest and complained loudly, our voices echoing down the canyon. I thought he would throw something at us. But instead, he just stared. Disappearing inside the house, he returned with a flat rock covered with pieces of something. He laid it on top of the stone wall that surrounded the estate then retreated to his seat.

"What do you think?" my mate asked. "Is it safe?"

"Stay here and keep watch," I told her. "If he makes a move toward me, swoop down and give him a good peck. If he stays put, come join me."

I flew from our tree and landed on the wall, croaking softly and watching the man. He leaned back, his mouth split open, showing teeth. I edged toward the flat rock, bobbing and weaving across the top of the wall. I smelled the food. The man didn't move. I had devoured half of it before my mate joined me. We gobbled the rest, savoring the sweet taste of fruits that the humans often left behind in the side canyons where they lived in cloth houses and huddled around fires at night.

When we finished we flew to our nest. The man held some kind of machine to his eyes and pointed it at us. A soft click, click, click broke the mid-afternoon stillness. The brown woman joined him. She leaned forward and pressed her face against his. They sat together, face-to-face, and made low sounds. My mate dug me in the shoulder with her beak and flew out over the town toward the seaside rocks where pelicans and cormorants gathered to dry their wings in the afternoon sun. We danced and spun in the air, riding the currents. I flew upside-down with my claws linked with hers and cried out to other ravens. We didn't return to our tree until the sun dipped below the ridgeline and the cold settled in.

Seasons passed. The brown woman grew large and then a little human joined the pair. The man continued putting out plates of food every day and my mate and I grew heavy. She hatched many chicks until last spring when she stopped. Another small one joined the man and woman. On warm afternoons, adult humans crowded the yard, drank much amber liquid, and ate until late at night, being more raucous than any of us ravens could ever be. On one afternoon, the man placed chunks of meat over a fire. The other humans stood back from the pit and away from its smoke.

"Look what he's laying out for us," my mate said.

"There's too many of them around for us to try," I said.

"Ah, come on. We're ravens. We can do what we want. I'll perch on the roof and start croaking while you grab some meat."

I always knew my mate had a loud call; but that day she outdid herself. All the humans stopped what they were doing and stared at her, spreading their mouths and showing teeth. I flew high above the estate and dove at a steep angle toward the fire pit. At the last moment, I stuck out my legs and braked with fluttering wings. Landing on the edge of the pit, I leaned forward, stabbed a chunk of meat, and I took off. It felt hot and smelled delicious. The man ran toward me, his mouth open and complaining. I flapped hard and managed to climb to our nest where my mate joined me. A loud roar rose up from the crowd below. They lifted their glasses of amber and clear liquid into the air. We ate well that night and didn't fly the whole next day.

The little humans grew bigger. They left the estate each morning and returned in the afternoon. The man's hair turned silver and he slept most afternoons in the yard, winter and summer, with his blinking window machine and his bottles. Sometimes the brown woman would join him and they would call loudly to each other. Once he reached out and struck her across the face and she ran from his grasping claws. We didn't see her for days. But our food plates kept coming and we decorated our nest with pieces of cloth swiped from the couple's outdoor tables, scraps of pretty paper left from their gatherings, and fur from their fat tomcat. We had fun gently pulling out clumps of his soft gray coat while he lay sleeping in the sun. If we kept quiet, he wouldn't even wake.

One evening, I woke from my nap to the sound of a large yellow machine with a light on its roof rumbling on the road next to the estate. The sun had dropped below the canyon ridge and the sky would soon be black.

"What's going on?" my mate asked.

"Someone must be leaving," I said. "Anytime one of those machines shows up someone leaves... or arrives."

In the yard, the man and his brown mate called loudly to each other. The little ones clutched her blue-green dress and made strange whining sounds. The woman's face looked wet and glistening, just like the small ones, like they had all been caught in a thunderstorm. At her feet rested boxy things with handles. The pair's cries grew louder. The woman moved to the far edge of the yard, pulled something from one of her claws, something gold with a bright flash. She flung it into the dark canyon below. Grabbing the boxy things, she herded the little ones before her and they all climbed into the yellow machine. It rolled downhill to the ferry landing.

"What do you think that was all… "I began to ask. But my mate had flown from our tree and dove down the canyon, disappearing into the black shadows. I called to her but got no reply. I waited. The light had almost disappeared before I heard the whoosh of her wings.

"Where did you go? I was…" I stopped speaking. In her beak she held a gold ring with shiny pieces of glass attached to it.

"I couldn't leave it down there," she said, her whole body shaking.

"It is pretty. But why go to all that trouble?"

"I don't know. I just have a feeling that it's important." She pressed the ring into the side of our nest, right above a piece of yellow cloth, where the morning sun would catch it and make it gleam brightly.

For days we didn't see the man. A strange old woman came from the house each morning and placed our food on top of the wall. The rains came and when the man finally returned to the yard, he sat in his chair and stared across the channel at the mainland while draining bottles of amber liquid. But when the sky brightened and the yellow coreopsis bloomed across the hillsides, he seemed to change. He drank from a clear bottle that he carried with him everywhere. During the day, my mate and I found him running along the ridge trails above the town, his body wet and glistening. He became slim, spent afternoons pounding madly on the window machine's panel until darkness came. He showed his teeth a lot when he talked with other humans and always pointed us out to his friends.

One summer afternoon, a yellow machine pulled up to the estate and the brown woman and the two little ones climbed out. The man met them outside the main building. They moved to the yard and he sat with the woman. They linked claws while the little ones played in the fountain and chased each other in and out of the house, calling loudly, their voices high and burbling like the canyon creek after a storm. The man pressed his face against her face. They stayed that way for a long time.

With a flurry of action, my mate snatched the gold ring with its bright glass from the wall of our nest and soared upward into the darkening sky. I followed her, my shoulders aching from the effort and from age. We circled the humans in the yard. I called loudly until they looked up at us. My mate dove toward them and I followed. With a flutter of wings we landed on the table. They stared at us, open-mouthed. My mate waddled forward and dropped the ring from her beak in front of the woman.

Tracks of water glistened down the woman's face. She picked up the ring. Her mouth spread wide, showing teeth. The pair made little coughing sounds.

We rose into the cool night, both of us struggling with the effort, and flew circles over the estate, croaking and watching the humans wave at us until the light failed.

"I knew she would want it back," my mate said.

"You always were a romantic," I replied, clacking my beak loudly at her.

We headed up canyon, black birds flying in a black night, and joined our aging brethren in the trees along the ridge road near the reservoir. We would share our stories with the others, let a young pair of ravens take over our nest, and wait until the time for our final flights.

66.
Underview
A.J. Huffman

Frozen breath builds
bridges to everywhere.
Pale stalagmites,
silent as skyscrapers
and fragile as reflections
of fate, waver in the embrace
of windless shadow.

67.
Visiting Aunt Mae
Kerry E.B. Black

Erin sniffed back snot bubbles. Winter clung to the air, refusing spring to thaw her saddened heart. She pulled her hoodie tight, but a geyser of ice threatened to explode within.

It's all too much. School. Bullies. Growing up. Mom and Dad.

Marlin. Her heart dropped when she thought of her cousin. She swiped tears and paid little attention as she progressed past the school bus stop through neighborhoods she trick-or-treated in with her parents. She pushed out her chin, defiant, and ignored the goody-two-shoes voice nagging inside her head.

Birds chattered, unimpeded, as she marched along sidewalks peppered with emerging spring flowers. She turned up the gated drive, surprising herself.

Guess I meant to come here.

She knew the way. Second turn-off from the main drag, under a big oak tree. Daddy held her right hand and Marlin's left not long ago. She read the names carved in granite until she found her. Mae. Beloved Wife and Mother. The dates of her birth and death.

The words did nothing to describe Aunt Mae's vibrant personality. It left out how photo shy she was, or the way she held her cards, or how her voice tickled when she whispered in Erin's ear. It neglected bedtime stories and prayers and snuggles on couches. Aunt Mae understood kids. She seemed like one herself sometimes.

Erin drooped to the hard ground and hugged her knees to her chest. No grass grew on the fresh grave. The funeral flowers decayed atop the churned earth, like a memory frozen.

Her internal geyser erupted, and tears raced, unchecked, into her jean. Sobs wracked her, and she rocked back and forth in remembrance of childhood comforts.

"Aunt Mae, I know you are probably relaxing in Heaven, but it is a real mess here since you left. Everyone knows it, but no one will talk about it. Marlin is living with us. Thought you might want to know if you didn't. His dad's gone kinda crazy since you, well, since you left."

Wonder why I called him Marlin's Dad, not Uncle? She pushed that aside.

"He's not doing so great." She thought of the changes in her best friend. "He mopes around and won't play. He doesn't care about school or bathing or anything really. I think he misses you. I know I do," she sniffed. "I think Marlin wants his Dad back, too. It's like he lost both of you when you, when you, died." The word fell like a tombstone from her lips.

Her vision steadied. Deep breaths.

Erin ignored wheels crunching the gravel path. She pictured Aunt Mae's smile and big, blinking eyes hiding behind glasses and long bangs.

She startled. Her mother squatted behind her, wrapping Erin in an embrace. "Mom, I'm sorry. I just needed to talk to Aunt Mae."

Her mom lifted Erin into a hug, as though she were a toddler with long, dangling legs. "I understand. Are you done?"

Erin nodded against her mother's shaking shoulder. Her mom kissed her wet cheek. "Let's go then."

Erin held her mom's hand as they walked to the car. Dad looked cross behind the driver's wheel. Marlin scowled from the back seat. Erin halted, tugging at her mother's arm. "I'm sorry. I'm sorry I crossed streets without you. I left without telling you. I yelled."

Her mom leaned over her. "We worried, but I'm glad you're safe. Let's get home and warm up. We can talk more there."

Erin nodded but suspected they would forget the talk before they parked in their driveway.

68.
We Chat
Sarah Z. Sleeper

Angel messaged her right when she got online. "Hey." She stared at the screen, deciding how to respond. Should she say, "Hey" back and then wait to see what Angel said? Maybe she should say, "Hola," to show how she was studying Spanish at school. No, wait, that might be insulting, Angel was Mexican, after all. Isn't it insulting to try to speak a language not-your-own to someone who speaks it? Okay, she'd just say, "Hey." That was safest.

"What's up?" he typed in reply.

Nothing's up. Duh, I'm just chatting with you, just got home from school, like you. Boys are so stupid. She despised them, or most of them. Angel was stupid too, of course, but less stupid than most boys, and at least he was tall and wore clean t-shirts, not the grass-and-mayonnaise-stained shirts the boys in her grade wore.

"Nothing. Homework." That was a lie, but just a white one, not a real one. She'd start on her homework soon, before her mom got back and came in to her room to check. So annoying, her mother examining her computer several times each afternoon after school, making sure homework was on the screen, math problems or English paragraphs or chemistry notes. What did she think would be on there? Pornography? Gross.

She heard the garage door slam, paper bags rustling in the kitchen. She clicked off the chat program and opened her Spanish homework, a worksheet of words she must translate. "Maggie! Come help me," her mother yelled down the hall.

Maggie and her mom put away the fresh vegetables, the cereal and granola bar boxes, the green juice bottles, while Charlie watched from his bed near the laundry room door. They talked over Maggie's day at school, the mac-and-cheese with broccoli she'd had for lunch, tennis practice (she'd made all her serves), the silly crush that Cara had on David. "Do you like David too?" Her mom was always fishing, trying to find things out. Things that didn't exist.

"No. I don't like boys. You know that." Maggie knew that sarcasm wasn't the right way to talk to her mom, but was glad her mom didn't call her on it, just let it pass.

"Okay, well stay off of WeChat tonight. If you finish your homework, read your book."

Sure, that's what I'll do. Just homework. I won't paint my toenails or look up Ukraine online (Where is Ukraine? Why is Russia stealing it?), chat with any friends or think about anything other than homework. That'll make me a well-rounded person, acceptable to good colleges. That's just what I'll do.

Back in her bedroom she clicked on WeChat and Angel was still there. "Maggie?" he'd typed, fifteen minutes earlier, while she was helping her mother. The tiny little words above the chat line showed her exactly when he'd sent the message. "Sent at 5:45." She knew he could also see when she read them because on his screen the word "Read" would appear, meaning he'd read her message.

"Hi Angel."

"Meet me for ice cream? Fifteen minutes?"

"HA! Ha ha!! Very funny." Why was he asking me that? She was in sixth grade, too young to go out meeting friends on her own. He knew that. Her parents would kill her if she walked the ten blocks to Coldstone by herself without letting them know. The neighborhood was safe, of course, and she walked Charlie around it each day, but to get to the ice cream shop she'd have to cross two busy streets and go into a strip mall. Besides, sixth graders and eighth graders don't meet up, don't hang out. It was dorky enough that Maggie and Angel were online friends. They never so much as said hello to each other at school. "Gotta go," she said.

"Geek! Too much time on homework," he said, and she clicked over to her Spanish assignment.

The next day at school Angel ignored her, as usual, and she ignored him back. Their lunch tables were right next to each other and she saw the giant, cheese-smothered burger he'd ordered. She thought she saw him notice the dainty, healthy salad she'd selected. Her mom had told her that only sloppy people eat pasta and sandwiches every day, that you had to eat veggies and salads too, otherwise you'd get FAT, and Maggie would die before she'd let herself get FAT. She was almost the skinniest girl in her class, except for Dominique, who took dance lessons for three hours every day and wanted to be a reality TV star. Maggie played tennis every day, had lessons twice per week, walked Charlie, which counted as exercise too, and anyway was naturally slender, like her mother.

Angel glanced at me when he left the lunchroom, didn't he? She was sure he did and she'd almost said hello, but then remembered that they don't talk in real life, just online. It was hard not to say hi to him. Maggie was a friendly person, all her teachers said so, "cheerful and helpful," Mrs. White had written on her semester evaluation. Not talking to Angel seemed opposite of her personality. But, they had some sort of pact. Online only.

Two days later Angel popped up on her screen, his selfie showed the just the collar of his blue t-shirt and the bottom of his grin, the rest of his face was cut off. "Maggie!"

She felt a ping in the pit of her stomach, something she'd felt at lunch that day when she was sure he smiled at her. 'Play it cool,' that's what Cara had told her. 'Don't act happy.' "Oh hey Angel."

"MAGGIE!" All caps and Angel was now yelling at her, insistent and bold. "Meet me for ice cream!!" Two exclamation points, definitely not cool. But nice. Nice that he was so excited to chat with her.

She heard her mother in the bedroom across the hall, on the phone with her dad. He lived a few blocks away with his new wife, Shelley, and Maggie went there on Fridays, along with Charlie, for the weekends. Her mom let her walk there since it was so close. The only people she encountered on her walks were neighbors, familiar faces that she'd seen for years, even if she often forgot their names.

"Not today," Maggie typed. "Friday." Right when she clicked send, she felt her face flush. Did I really intend to meet him at Coldstone on Friday? Could I? Sneak over during my Friday walk to Dad's? Her hands were shaking over the keyboard and she was disappointed in herself. Either she was lying to Angel, by saying she'd meet him. Or, she'd have to lie to her parents in order to squeeze in the time to veer over to the ice cream place during her walk. And if I did meet Angel, what in the world would I say? What do boys and girls talk about anyway? At school, most of the conversations she and her friends had with boys consisted of forced interactions as they commiserated on class projects, or oddly, the occasional boy who poked a girl in the side with his finger and kept on walking. Cara insisted those finger pokes actually meant that the boy liked the girl, an idea that Maggie thought sounded as stupid as the boys themselves. But her mom told her it was possible, that a boy might do an awkward thing like poke you when he likes you. She had also made Maggie promise to tell her if and when she liked a boy for the first time, but Maggie wasn't sure that was a good idea. Her mom couldn't always be trusted to keep her mouth shut, like the time she'd asked Cara about David, which let Cara know Maggie had spilled.

"K. Friday. TTYL." Angel's icon disappeared from Maggie's screen, but Cara's was now there.

"Hi. Just talked to Angel."

"Really!!?? What did he say?"

"We are meeting for ice cream."

"WHAT?!"

"I know."

"OMG. I KNEW he liked you."

"I know. I think I like him too. Don't tell anyone."

"OMG! OMG! OMG! I knew it. I knew that too."

"Sshhhhh."

Cara signed off with a winky face and that night Maggie couldn't sleep, fidgeting and going over in her mind what she might say to Angel. "Hi, Angel. Nice to see you." No, too formal. "Heya. How's it going, Angel?" Too forced. She settled on, "Hi, Angel." Just that, with no other words. After all, isn't it the boy's job to start the conversation, take the lead? Yes. "Hi, Angel" would be just right. He'd figure out what to say after that.

At lunch on Friday, Angel never looked her way at all, acted completely oblivious to her, and pretended that they weren't going to meet later. School got out early, an hour earlier than usual to accommodate parent-teacher meetings. Maggie's mom was there meeting with Mrs. White, so Cara's mom drove the girls home. Cara's squirmy, dirty little brother Jake was in front, and in the backseat the girls texted each other, excited about the meeting with Angel. "What if he tries to kiss you?"

"IDK!!!"

"I will spy on U!" And Maggie wished Cara could spy, so that if it became weird or awkward, she could give her some kind of signal and Cara would saunter over, act like she was at the ice cream shop by coincidence.

In her bedroom she packed her overnight backpack with her new pink and black butterfly PJs and her school books. She was glad she would get to see her dad, even if Shelley would be around too, and he'd told her he'd take her and Cara out for dinner at Bonjourno for her favorite pasta marinara, which she never ate around her mother. She stood still and took a few deep breaths before putting the leash on Charlie and starting toward Coldstone. It was a few blocks past her father's and she could make it back to his house without him ever knowing she hadn't gone directly there.

It was sunny and quiet, not even a dog barking for Charlie to bark back at. Until she got to the first busy road, she hadn't seen one car drive by. She crossed at the crosswalk and then at the next one. The strip mall was just to the left and she thought she saw Angel, standing on the sidewalk outside the ice cream shop. She felt a plonk in her stomach and her mouth was dry, but she was determined to be cool, smooth, nonchalant. As she got closer, she realized that the person on the sidewalk wasn't Angel, but someone she didn't know, a man with dark hair. Inside Coldstone, she saw three little boys licking cones as a mom paid the bill.

The man turned as she approached. "Maggie?"

Surprised that he knew her name, she said, "Yes."

"I'm Angel's father," he said, smiling a smile that resembled Angel's, she thought. He reached his hand down to Charlie, who sniffed and wagged. "I drove Angel over to meet you. He's on his phone right over there." He pointed toward a dark grey SUV with the back passenger door open. She saw Angel's leg sticking out of the door, the shoestrings untied on his blue hightops. He was so busy with his phone that he hadn't poked his head out or noticed that she was there. Annoying, typical. she thought. She was a little surprised that Angel had told his father about meeting her, but then again, maybe that was normal for eighth graders. They probably told their parents everything. Or, maybe just boys did, told their fathers anyway.

She took off her backpack and dropped it on the ground next to the car. No need to have it dig holes in her shoulders when she was talking to Angel. She secured Charlie's leash under the weight of the backpack and peeked into the car. "Angel?" she said, as her eyes struggled to adjust to the dim interior.

"Hi Maggie," said Angel, and she was surprised at how deep his voice was. She'd only heard him talk a few times, in passing at lunch, and couldn't quite remember what he sounded like.

She hadn't yet decided how to respond, when he reached forward and took both of her hands in his. Her throat caught and she couldn't say a word as he pulled her forward into the car and slammed the door behind her, just missing her foot. She saw that the man from the sidewalk was in the driver's seat and then the car lurched forward. When he finally came into focus, Maggie realized that Angel was not Angel after all.

Confused, she looked out the window and saw Charlie and her backpack on the pavement. Charlie stood as the car drove off and Maggie froze with fear. What would happen to Charlie? Would someone find him and take him home? Mom was going to ground me for sure and take away my computer.

The man who was not Angel gripped her arms hard, pushed her down onto the vinyl floormat. "Stop crying," he said, and slammed his knee into her jaw, which cracked with a sharp snap and a burst of pinpoint lights.

She squeezed her eyes shut. Through the swirling darkness on the back of her eyelids, her dad's face flashed into focus. Soft light emanated in blurry beams from his eyes into hers, ripple upon ripple of pulsing warmth. At the exact same moment, she saw her mother's beautiful smile, glowing with adoration, and she felt her strong hands holding and hugging her, infusing her with love, swaddling her clammy skin in a blanket of perfect comfort. All at once Maggie understood, though she'd made a grave mistake today, there would be no grounding, no punishment, and nothing else whatsoever at all.

69.
Winter Bizaré
A.J. Huffman

Frozen arrows. Sharper
showers of imperceptible nothing,
gone in a touch, a breath,
a quilt of captured dew.
This curtain of lace hangs
on the air, the ground,
the eyes, fortunate enough
to bare witness to
tomorrow's whiteness.

70.
Winter Nights
Alexandra Heep

A safe world resides
beneath my blankets
on cold winter nights.

No howling, stormy wind
no snow which drifts distinct
disturbs my universe below.

A safe world resides
beneath my blankets
on cold winter nights.

Thoughts are oh so warm
and dreams can do no harm
when I do stay below.

A safe world resides
beneath my blankets
on cold winter nights.

Cozy feelings abide
scary thoughts run and hide
from my sanctity below.

71.
Winter Wasting
A.J. Huffman

Snowflakes.
Fragile glitter,
silver suicides, rain.
Dissolve instantly against kiss
of skin.

72.
You O God of Abraham Are
Carmanie Bhatti

You O God of Abraham are
Forever kind, loving, gracious,
For your love rains through barriers
On us, who live through thick and thin

We who have different color,
Gifts and talents, possess the word
Of God, because the word does function
Sharper than a double-edged sword

Your power makes us embrace you
To hold on to your color of
Love, that we may be a witness
To the truth you are, to wear you

Being part of us you own us
Because you live, abide in us
And since we are in your embrace
We are called "Little Jesuses"

Let your love spill on us always
On our stains, that we are covered
With a new sheet of color, with
Identity as your children

Contributing Authors

A.J. Huffman

Where are you from?
Ormond Beach, Florida.

When and why did you begin writing?
Writing always just kind of came naturally to me. I wrote my first short story in grade school. It was about living in a yellow submarine with my pet fish. And I, of course, I wrote poetry in high school. But I didn't actually start taking my writing seriously until I got to college.

What would you say is your most interesting writing quirk?
I still prefer to write with a pen on paper. My writing friends think I'm nuts. They are all die-hard type straight to the screen computer writers.

What do you like to do when you're not writing?
Dude! I live in Florida! I'm at the beach!

As a child, what did you want to do when you grew up?
When I was a little girl I wanted to be a fashion designer. I was a total girly girl. I loved clothes and dresses and shoes. Oh wait, I still do, I just can't sew.

Alexandra Heep

Where are you from?
I was born and raised in Germany. I moved to the USA at age eighteen in 1986. I have lived in Michigan and Virginia, before settling in Chicago, Illinois.

When and why did you begin writing?
First I became a writer out of passion (in 2007), then the craft turned into necessity when I was laid off and became ill. It was the option for survival.

What would you say is your most interesting writing quirk?
English is my second language, so I tend to write too formal because I don't want people to know that. I also like using unusual words to describe simple actions, even when I just speak to someone.

What do you like to do when you're not writing?
Gardening and watching sports. I am also fascinated by weather and am a trained weather spotter.

As a child, what did you want to do when you grew up?
Mainly, to escape my childhood. I had no real ideas of what I wanted to "become" though. However, like a lot of children I wanted to be famous somehow.
www.aheepofeverything.blogspot.com

Carmanie Bhatti

I am an Urdu love poet and, an English theological poet. I was born and raised in Pakistan, and currently a seminary student in IL. I started writing Urdu poetry at the age of thirteen and later wrote English poetry as well. On my arrival in the US, in 2013, I won The Spine Book Poetry Competition, sponsored by ATLA, which stands for The American Theological Library Association. This competition required use of titles of books in libraries and write a theological poem, without using any article. In November 2014, The Young Writers' Forum, Murree, Pakistan endowed me with a Certificate of Honor for my Urdu poetry collection. This poetry was embedded in the light of theology.

I am also a photographer, a painter, an online reviewer for artists who are painters, photographers, short story writers and, poets. While I was in Pakistan, I translated the book *What Healthy Churches Do Right*, by David O Dykes. In 2013, it was published in Pakistan, with Urdu translation by me.

Ceiligh Cacho-Negrete

Ceiligh Cacho-Negrete loves reading, writing and winning at chess. She lives in Massachusetts with her parents and little sister. She is currently in 7th grade at the River Valley Middle School where she helped start a band, which is known far and wide - after all, 100 square feet is pretty big!   This is her first poem, but hopefully not her last.

Christopher Chagnon

Christopher Chagnon has written two bestselling novels; *The Dregs of Presque Isle* and *The Ghosts of Presque*, books one and two from the trilogy, *The Chandlerville Chronicles*. The third installment, *The Soldiers of Presque Isle*, will be released in spring of 2016. He is an award-winning short story writer and photographer living near Onaway, Michigan.

David Lee Featherman

Where are you from?

I grew up near Reading, Pennsylvania, and attended the former Shillington High School in John Updike's hometown. My father Wesley taught me algebra. Only much later did I learn that he was a centaur, thanks to his son.

When and why did you begin writing?

I've been learning the craft and writing fiction assiduously every day during the three years since my retirement, following more than four decades as an academic social scientist, university administrator, and foundation executive. Until now all my published writing was factual rather than imaginative, even when the empirical research started with "What if...?" In crafting fictional imagination, I relish exploring the spaces between those facts, being drawn into their rich possibilities and often unanticipated nuances of human encounters. It's a cool new challenge and places a much heavier burden upon the writer for evoking and sharing that discovery with others.

What would you say is your most interesting writing quirk?
I'm still too new at this to have developed a quirk.

What do you like to do when you're not writing?
I read, share story drafts and listen to music with my wife of nearly fifty years, and walk the dog—who is still agnostic about my literary musings.

As a child, what did you want to do when you grew up?
Too many things for a single lifetime, until college where I learned that I needed to winnow a bit. By default perhaps I chose to keep going to school and eventually to become a professor. I loved small seminars and probing young minds, but discovery through research became my single-minded passion on the job. At that point, I thought I had grown up. But now I think I'm only just getting there, as a grandfather and writer of fiction, with this my first literary publication.

Deborah Guzzi

Where are you from?
The land of Steven King.

When and why did you begin writing?
When I got a crayon.

What would you say is your most interesting writing quirk?
Sometimes I write with a cat zipped into my fleece sweatshirt.

What do you like to do when you're not writing?
Think about writing.

As a child, what did you want to do when you grew up?
I wanted to be a teacher. I teach on *Poetry Soup* often in blogs.

Diana Kathryn Plopa

Diana Kathryn is the associate publisher and editor in chief of Grey Wolfe Publishing. When she's not helping others publish their work, she diligently works on her own writing.

Diana Kathryn has written a collection of poetry, *Ideate Avail (2008)*, a memoir, *Wolfe Cub (2013)*, a novel, *Free Will (2014)*, and has contributed to the *Encore Writers* anthology (2015).

Diana Kathryn is currently collaborating with her muse, Drake the Duck, on a children's book, *The Griffin of Greed* and another novel, *A Tryst of Fate*; both of which will be released in early 2016. She and Drake also have six other writing projects in various stages of completion.

Elizabeth Farney Maxson

Where are you from?
I am originally from Dayton, Ohio.

When and why did you begin writing?
I began writing when I was in grade school. I was never very good in art, so I was the kid who asked to write a paper, poem, or story instead of using scissors and glue.

What would you say is your most interesting writing quirk?
I like to revise. I like rereading work and trying to make sure that each word is exactly what I want.

What do you like to do when you're not writing?
When I am not writing, I park hop with my children Isaac (3) and Darcy (10). I also teach ZUMBA, choreograph/direct musicals, teach dance, read, and teach high school English.

As a child, what did you want to do when you grew up?
When I was child, among other professions, I wanted to be the first woman Cincinnati Reds player. I also wanted to be a Rockette and a lawyer.

Heath Bowen

Heath Bowen is an arising contemporary poet whose work will appear in the upcoming issues of *Muddy River Poetry Review* and *Eskimo Pie*. Heath has an MFA from Spalding University. He has worked years at *The Louisville Review* as an editor. Heath is an English teacher and a studio musician who currently resides in New Albany, Indiana with his wife and daughter.

John Grey

John Grey is Australian born short story writer, poet, playwright, musician, Providence RI resident since late seventies. . Has been published in numerous magazines including *Weird Tales*, *Christian Science Monitor*, *Greensboro Poetry Review*, *Poem*, *Agni*, *Poet Lore* and *Journal Of The American Medical Association* as well as the horror anthology *What Fears Becom* and the science fiction anthology *Futuredaze*. Has had plays produced in Los Angeles and off-off Broadway in New York. Winner of the *Rhysling Award* for short genre poetry in 1999.

Jon Moray

Jon Moray has been writing short stories for six years and has been published in several print and online markets. When not working and being a devoted father, he enjoys running and playing basketball.

Kerry E.B. Black

Where are you from?
I grew up on the edge of woods filled with mysteries. Now, I raise my family along a fog-covered river that feeds into the mighty Mississippi.

When and why did you begin writing?
As a child, I wrote for the younger children at my school. My mother is an amazing writer with a wild and active imagination. I suppose I inherited her love for the written word.

What would you say is your most interesting writing quirk?
I feel bereft and unfulfilled when not writing.

What do you like to do when you're not writing?
I love spending time with my amazing family. Holidays are my absolute favorite, and I seize any opportunity to celebrate. Travel is a great passion of mine as well.

As a child, what did you want to do when you grew up?
I wanted to be a jockey, but alas, I had a growth spurt that put me out of the running. I do hope to see the Kentucky Derby someday, though, and feel the thoroughbred's hooves thundering around the track in person.

Mark Hudson

Mark Hudson is an author who spends of time reading, writing, and doing art. He recently read of someone who likes to get up early and write, like a lot of writers, and he has found that his best ideas come to him early with really strong coffee. He gets published periodically in different print magazines and on-line, but finds Grey Wolfe Publishing has published more of his pieces than anyone else. Mark has relatives in Michigan, and one time he was reading one of the stories in one of the anthologies about an author reflecting on a Michigan childhood, camping, picnicking, inviting friends over to join in hot dogs with families, etc. Mark was almost jealous at how kind everyone seemed in the Michigan story. He told his aunt and uncle this this weekend, and his aunt said, "Yes, that was how my childhood was in Michigan."

As Mark sits here in the library writing this bio, he overhears a librarian and a patron discussing the latest local news event of a Chicago cop killing a teen and longs for a better world. Writing is sometimes Mark's only escape.

M.F. Nagel

M.F. Nagel was born in anchorage Alaska. Her Athabaskan and Eyak heritage gave her a love of poetry. M.F. now lives and writes near the banks of the Matanuska River in the Palmer Butte, Alaska, where the moose, wild dog roses and salmonberries provide unending joy and inspiration.

Michael D. Jones

Michael D. Jones has a Master of Arts degree in English from Oakland University, and a Bachelor of Arts degree in English and Communications from the University of Michigan. His recently published first book length collection, *Unlikely Trees* (2014), gathers "God and family and nature into a set of reflections that deliver the breadth of one life into a complete impression." An appraiser for over twenty years, nonprofit development professional, husband and father of four, he lives in Holland, Michigan.

Priya Vannapusa

Where are you from?
Michigan.

When and why did you begin writing?
High School contributed to School Magazine.

What would you say is your most interesting writing quirk?
Day dreaming about it until I can see it clearly before it takes shape
on paper.

What do you like to do when you're not writing?
Read, read ,read.

As a child, what did you want to do when you grew up?
Be a lawyer.

Shannon Waite

Where are you from?
I grew up in Warren, Michigan, which is where I still live to this day. I love the city and this area of the state.

When and why did you begin writing?
Is that even a question? Since I could hold a pencil, I've been writing and drawing. I've always enjoyed creating and I can't remember a time that I wasn't doing it. I'm in love with words, and that fascination has only grown over the years.

What would you say is your most interesting writing quirk?
My most interesting writing quick would have to be poetic prose; I had always written stories when I was younger, and then in high school I focused on poetry. When I transitioned back into storytelling, my poetry bled into the work.

What do you like to do when you're not writing?
If I'm not writing, I'm managing a handful of high schoolers (I'm a teacher), I'm raising hamsters, drinking banana milkshakes, reading, and going on long walks.

As a child, what did you want to do when you grew up?
The list: singer, doctor, vet, writer, president, and probably a few other things. All at once. Then I decided psychologist, and that lasted for four years in high school, then second semester of senior year I vetoed that and decided to be a high school English teacher.

Tara Johnson

Where are you from?
I am from Cambidge, Ontario, Canada..

When and why did you begin writing?
I started writing when I was eleven years old because I enjoy telling stories.

What would you say is your most interesting writing quirk?
When I get an idea, I play Majong on the computer for hours seeing the story in my head like a movie and this helps me to feel the emotions of the characters.

What do you like to do when you're not writing?
I like to read and play my keyboard.

As a child, what did you want to do when you grew up?
For a period of time, I wanted to be a lawyer.

Terry Sanville

Terry Sanville lives in San Luis Obispo, California with his artist-poet wife (his in-house editor) and one plump cat (his in-house critic). He writes full time, producing short stories, essays, poems, and novels. Since 2005, his short stories have been accepted by more than 210 literary and commercial journals, magazines, and anthologies including *The Potomac Review*, *The Bitter Oleander*, *Shenandoah*, and *Conclave: A Journal of Character*. He was nominated twice for a Pushcart Prize for his stories *The Sweeper* and *The Garage*. Terry is a retired urban planner and an accomplished jazz and blues guitarist – who once played with a symphony orchestra backing up jazz legend George Shearing.

Tyler Lentz

Tyler Lentz is a graphic design student at the Art Institute of Michigan. When he is not working on design projects, he likes to read and spend time outside. Done is Tyler's first published piece.